Christmas with the Horned God

Aveda Vice

Bad Bite LLC

Also By Aveda Vice

Dedication

Chase what you want, or catch what you're afraid of.

Author's Note

This book contains sexual situations. It is not intended for anyone under the legal age of adulthood. All characters depicted in sexual situations herein are over 18 years of age. This book is not to be used as an informational guide to any type of sex or sexual education.

Some topics within this book may be sensitive or disturbing to some readers. Reader discretion is advised.

For detailed information on the topics addressed, please visit the author's website or scan the codes below.

One

Rowen

Not answering the phone will be worse. Not answering the phone will cause more problems.

Still, Rowen's finger twitches over the red *Dismiss Call* button. Her car speakers keep ringing. A timid voice speaks up in the back of her mind. *You don't have to answer. Call back later. Say you're driving! It's true!*

Any reasoning is drowned out by guilt. Answering will be easier. Answering will keep things harmonious. It's the least she can do, given the circumstances. "Mom, I'm driv-"

"Have you left yet?" Her mother's voice surrounds her, loud and tinny.

Rowen turns down the volume with a wince. "Yes, Mom. I texted you; I'm on the road. There's snow, so I need to foc-"

"Because you know how you are. I never know if you've *actually* left, or if I'm going to be stuck waiting around for you."

Rowen's teeth dig into her lip. *That's not me*, she wants to say. *That's you. You do that.* But she keeps quiet as she guides the car along the mountain road.

"What time will you be here?" her mother asks.

"I texted..." Rowen trails off. *Just answer the question. It's easier. Be polite.* "Around four."

"*Really?*"

Rowen braces herself. She knows this voice well, a different pitch from her mother's typical irritation. This tone is disappointed, resembling a petulant child.

"I thought you were going to be here for lunch."

Restlessly, Rowen fiddles with her hair and musters as much chipperness as she can. "Unfortunately not." An errant, light brown strand falls into her vision, and she tucks it hastily away. *Eyes on the road, Rowen.* "I told you I wouldn't make it for lunch when you called earlier this week. Remember?"

"I don't remember that."

Pursing her lips, Rowen nods to keep her frustration inside. Her mother never remembers any of her own mistakes — only Rowen's.

"This is very inconsiderate of you, Rowen," her mother sighs. "I already invited the Hastings over for brunch. For *you*. Remember their son, the one taking over the family business? Now you're going to be wasting his time."

Rowen's pale fingers tighten around the steering wheel. "I told you —" Her voice wavers. She doesn't say she never asked to be set up. She doesn't point out that brunch would still be too early, even if they *had* agreed Rowen would arrive at lunchtime. Instead, she exhales and follows the path of least resistance. "I'm not really looking to date right now. I'll be so busy taking care of you, and I actually just got a promotion at work..."

She holds her breath to leave space for her mother's response. This is the job her mother encouraged — *insisted* — she pursue, despite Rowen's quiet misery in cubicles. And Rowen made it work, despite the stuffy blouses and fluorescent lights and passionless data entry.

A foolish decision. Her mother sighs again, and Rowen pictures her pinching the bridge of her nose. "I told you, work will never fulfill you the way a family will — the way *kids* will — and you can't have those without a husband. I mean, for goodness' sake, your cousin just got married, and she's five years younger than you."

Shame creeps up Rowen's neck as she swallows the words crowding her mouth. *You don't need a husband for that. And you told me to focus on my career. You told me never to rely on a man, because he'll leave just like Dad.* Her stomach sours. Rolling down her window, she lifts her face toward the brisk air and dabs at the sweat on her cheeks. Dammit, she's going to ruin her makeup. Her mother will point it out. Her mother will —

"Hello?" Her mother's voice rises above the wind. "Are you still there?"

Mournfully, Rowen watches the glass roll back up. It's stifling in this car. Her voice is weak. "I told you, I don't think I want kids —"

"Don't say that," her mother hisses. "God help me, Rowen, I barely ask for anything. After all I've done for you, you could at least find a nice man to give me grandkids before I *die*."

Rowen flinches. It's not as if she can correct her mother. Her mother *is* sick; that's why Rowen's taken a sabbatical. Granted, she hasn't been able to get any details about what exactly her mother is afflicted with. *Incurable*, her mother said. *Miserable appointments. I wouldn't be surprised if it kills me.*

Sweat pricks the back of Rowen's thick thighs. Surely her mother is exaggerating. Rowen doesn't want to think about what it would mean if she isn't. It would change Rowen's life. It would make her feel...

God, Rowen: how are you thinking about yourself at a time like this? Abashed, she shakes the thoughts from her head. Once she gets to her mother's house, she'll figure out what they're dealing with. She'll make a plan. She'll figure out a way to get back to her life.

Fortunately, her mother hasn't noticed her silence. Unfortunately, she's still stuck on the same topic. "You'll regret not having kids. Once you change your mind, then where will you be? You're already cutting it close. In a few more years, you'll be thirty-five, and you know what they say about high-risk pregnancies..."

Rowen's shoulders hike toward her shoulders as her mind drifts off. Even without her mother physically present, Rowen's body knows how to respond. Keeping herself small, as if taking up less space will pacify the situation. Avoiding eye-contact, in case it sets her mother off even further.

Strange how Rowen has spent so much time learning to placate her mother, yet it still feels out of her control...but she keeps trying in hopes that it will pacify her mother. Impress her. Make her proud, for *once.*

It never works.

"...And you never spend time with your family anymore," her mother groans. Rowen pictures her draped across a chaise, the back of one hand flung across her forehead. "It's been a year since you last came home. Monthly phone calls don't cut it, Rowen. Most girls call their mother every day to talk about things."

The thought makes Rowen's chest tight. Even monthly calls are too much for her. One visit a year saps all her energy. Before the diagnosis, she'd been pulling away from her mother, getting this new job and brand new apartment. But now...

Any fight Rowen has trickles out of her like a slow leak. Her body's already leaden from this brief conversation. Every interaction feels like drawing plays on a white board, strategizing which words and phrases will keep things from spiraling out of control. Nothing will please her mother, but at least Rowen can mitigate the turmoil.

"I'll be there later today." Rowen's pleasant voice hides the weariness. "And I'm staying with you for a few months, remember?"

Her mother sighs wistfully. "I guess we'll get one last good Christmas before..."

"Jesus, Mom," Rowen mutters.

"What was that?"

Rowen's teeth clench. "I said, I'll see you soon."

She slams the *End Call* button before guilt consumes her. Her mother won't be happy that she didn't say goodbye. Rowen can already hear the inevitable. *Don't be disrespectful. So help me, Rowen...*

Fearfully, she holds down the power button until the screen turns black.

In its darkness, she sees the reflection of her round cheeks, ruddy from her tiny act of rebellion. She cranks up the AC and tries to formulate a plan. She'll tell her mother she went through a spotty patch of service. If the Hastings are there when Rowen arrives, her mother won't make a scene. Rowen will get a few merciful hours of silent glares and underhanded comments.

See? Easy.

An ache forms at the front of her head. Headaches are no stranger to her after years of biting her tongue and gritting her teeth. This visit with her mother hasn't even started, and Rowen's body is already revolting.

She squints against the pain. There are hours of driving

left, and she desperately needs a distraction. Rifling through her center console, she searches for an abandoned audiobook or misplaced CD. Maybe she could turn on the radio, but it'll lose connection soon...

Her fingers brush something sleek and metallic inside the console. Victorious, she drags it out by the hole in the center. The CD is covered in various shades of permanent marker, doodles and handwriting that jerk her into the past.

It's been years since she last saw this mix. It should have been even longer, but Rowen couldn't bring herself to get rid of the keepsake when she bought this car. Instead, she slipped the CD out of sight like a security blanket she couldn't bear to look at, left in the dusty attic of her memories.

Multicolors glint across her dash. Even with the sun behind a wall of gray clouds, this CD finds a way to spread its light. Carefully, she slips the disc into the player. A familiar drum cadence filters through the speakers, and her lips curl into a fond smile.

At least the maker of this CD didn't hear her phone call. That's the only person who would have told Rowen the ugly truth. *Your people-pleasing is pathological, princess. Stand up for once. Either chase what you want, or catch what you're afraid of.*

But that voice has been as lost to her as this CD, leaving her to sink further and further into her eagerness to please. Everyone around her seems to love it. Every boss admires her willingness to stay late when no one else will. Every first date compliments what a great listener she is, unaware that none of them have asked her a question in hours. Every "friend" thanks her for being so understanding when they ask her to go out of her way.

Rowen's jaw tightens. It's not so easy to stand up for herself when everyone prefers her lying down.

As she rounds a curve of the mountain, a billboard leans

decrepit behind the guardrail. Its red-and-green images are torn on a faded snowy background. Rowen squints. Is that smudge next to Santa's sleigh a person or a deer? Beneath the cutesy image are sun-bleached words: *Escape to the Christmas Tree Lodge. Last exit. 1 mile ahead.*

Her chest twinges. She didn't realize she was this close to her old job. It's been years since she worked on the mountain for the winter. When was the last time she traveled through here? It must have been back in college, the same year she last saw...

Her eyes dart to the rearview, as if her mother might appear behind her. There's nothing but snowdrifts and another mile marker fading in the distance.

Dread settles into her body. That's how her entire life feels. Her, driving down a long highway and watching the exits pass her by. She isn't even in the driver's seat. She's strapped in the back, too scared to grab the steering wheel of her own life. There's always someone else to take over, her mother or bosses or boyfriends guiding her through events that she's only a passenger of.

It feels like she's coming up on the last opportunity to change course, the final exit before an endless stretch of highway. No U turns, no rest stops, nothing but the road she'll never be able to turn off of.

As she comes around the bend, that highway stretches out before her. It continues straight through the mountains toward her mother's house...but a narrower road curves up into the trees, disappearing between pine branches and snow.

Rowen's teeth dig into her lip. She just needs a break. A detour. A pitstop to *breathe*. Then she'll continue toward her mother's house and spend the next few days, weeks, months caring for her. Taking the side road will add a little bit of time to her journey, but she'll still get to her mother's before dark. Hell, maybe her mother will go to bed early to make a point, and Rowen can slip in unnoticed.

An alt-rock anthem blasts through the speakers, the sharp strum of the guitar urging Rowen on. With one last glance in her side mirrors, she cranks the volume and turns off the main road.

Rowen

Unfortunately, the backroads of the mountain aren't as well-paved as Rowen remembers. Her car jostles along, avoiding potholes and patches of snow. There are no other cars on the narrow road, and the few old houses or businesses look shut-down or abandoned. Boards cover windows, roofs and porches fallen into disrepair as withered plants grow over railings. Part of the Christmas tree farm's charm was its remote location, but now, this place feels…isolated.

Words are sprayed in fluorescent orange paint on the last house she passes. Squinting, she manages to make them out.

Beware wildlife! Unnatural!

An uncertain chill crawls up her spine. 'Unnatural'? What does that mean? The timid voice starts in her head again.

That's why you should've stayed on the main road. That's why you should've —

She shuts it down, doing her best to ignore her disappointment. Maybe the tree farm has been abandoned, too. It's been years since she's been back, but something always felt magical about this place. Her last season here was the last time she felt any Christmas spirit, and it had been...enchanting. Powerful. Real.

Maybe she was hoping to find some of that again, but she'll have to make do with a simple look. Once she reminisces over the view, she'll get back to the real world...and her mother. Begrudgingly, Rowen turns her phone back on and pulls up to the short, covered bridge at the edge of the property.

Its dark wood is weathered, but still stable. On the other side, the long, dirt driveway is covered with snow. There's no sign of activity, not even a snowplow or a shovel.

Her chest deflates. So much for her rebellion. There's no way her car will make it through the thick drifts to the top of the hill. The farm really must be abandoned.

At least she can get a look at it from the bridge. She puts her car in park, stepping out into the cold and tugging her trench coat closed. When she lifts her nose and inhales, brisk air fills her lungs, a stinging reminder of exactly what she missed about this place. She steps onto the bridge, glancing over the railing as the wood creaks. There's a steep dropoff, at least twenty-five feet to the stream below...but the bridge stands firm.

On the other embankment, the weathered drive continues through a forest on either side. Eventually, those trees peter out and open to a steep hill that used to be covered in evergreens. As Rowen reaches the middle of the bridge, the rest of the hill comes into view. The bottom is clear and empty, but at the top, conifer trees grow wild and free as they stretch toward the overcast sky. It's as picturesque as she remembers, a greeting card of snow-covered firs surrounding the lodge peeking out at the top.

Something growls behind her.

Whirling, she clutches her keys between her fingers. There's nothing on the bridge. Nothing next to her car. Nothing on the vertical embankment. Instinctively, she takes another step back —

Hooves beat against the ground. Rowen barely has time to turn toward the forest before a herd of deer stampedes toward her. Antlers scrape the ceiling of the bridge, planks trembling beneath her feet. There's nowhere to run. She clasps her arms overhead, prepared to be slammed against the railing —

Wind whips past her, body jostled from side to side. She stays frozen, her heartbeat thudding over everything else. Only after a long moment of silence does she lift her head and find only tracks in the snow.

Beneath her, the bridge groans and shifts. Snow tumbles off the roof as it sinks, half-blocking the view of her car. She stumbles against the railing, pushing off toward the nearest solid ground and skidding to her knees on the dirt road.

The bridge crumbles behind her.

Breath puffs between her lips, mind whirring as she tries to collect her thoughts. Her car is on the other side of the embankment. There's no way she can cross the steep ravine, even if it weren't an icy deathtrap. No one knows she's here. There wasn't another living soul on the drive up, and cold is already seeping through her socks.

Panic bubbles inside her. She forces the feeling down, swiping at her nose in hopes the cold pain will keep her head on straight. *Think, Rowen.* There's another bridge half a mile down. It'll take a little bit of walking, but she can get back to her car...

And away from whatever is happening out here. What was that growling? What was up with those deer? Her mind flashes back to the painted sign: *Beware wildlife! Unnatural!*

Unnatural, indeed. She hadn't gotten a good look at any of the herd, but they seemed to come out of nowhere. Had they been spooked by something?

She turns toward the dirt road, surrounded on both sides by deciduous trees. The oaks and maples lost their leaves long ago, but the forest is still dense with evergreens and holly bushes breaking up the white landscape.

Something hangs from a nearby tree. Hesitantly, Rowen steps closer, pushing back a fir branch to get a better look.

A stag sways in the wind, back legs bound high as its forelegs stretch toward the ground. Her heart jolts, making her stumble back. Maybe it's stuck...but when it rotates, its chest and stomach are flayed open in a gory display. There is no clean slice. Whatever tore it open was feral, ripping away entire chunks of flesh to leave bone and tendon exposed.

Her stomach turns. The marks are too vicious to be human, but from the way it's strung up...no animal put it there.

Her chest tightens, breathing shallow and fast. She covers her nose, even though she smells nothing from the decayed flesh. *It's just a deer. Someone was hunting. Don't freak out. Don't —*

A rifle cocks. "This is private property."

She bites back a curse, spinning toward the voice. The owner is only a few meters away, angling the gun toward the sky. It's little reassurance. With only a slight movement, the barrel could swing back toward her...

Her heart hammers. "I didn't — know anyone else was here."

The stranger hikes a brow. "Is that the only thing stopping you from trespassing?"

God help her, she wants to laugh just to expel the nerves buzzing through her body. Her voice isn't working. All her fear-addled mind can come up with is "handsome." *Handsome stranger. Handsome scowl.* Good lord, is this the mush her mind turns to when she's about to die?

As if the stranger can read her thoughts, they glare without a hint of amusement...until something else passes over their face. "Rowen."

It's odd hearing her name in this familiar setting mixed with the strangeness of everything else. It doesn't register that this person shouldn't know her as she gestures to the hill in the distance. "I was just stopping by. I used to work here —"

"Rowen." Frustrated, the stranger uncocks the rifle. "It's me."

They speak as if she should recognize them. Adrenaline courses through her body with no outlet, her teeth chattering as she tucks her arms around herself. How do they know her name? She's certain she's never seen them before...but when her eyes narrow, she recognizes the bright green of theirs. The full bow of their top lip. The broad expanse of their nose.

It's the creator of her mixtape, summoned from her memories and into reality. Her mouth opens around a familiar name —

Before she can begin, the "stranger" cuts her off. "It's Asher, now. 'They.' I'm sure that big city job taught you all about pronouns."

A surprised laugh jumps into her throat. Their body may look different, but their dry wit has only sharpened. Rowen fits her lips around their name. "Asher. Wow..." Thoughts dogpile her, memories searing into her stomach as she tries to form a sensible sentence. "You're so...I'm still 'she.' Wow, you look..."

A lot different than when I left you. It's a suckerpunch of a reminder of the last time they spoke — the last time they *fought.* Her face burns. Maybe Asher will think she's chapped from the wind. They certainly don't have that problem, the peachy, sun-kissed skin of their face seemingly used to harsh weather. Part of their dark brown hair is pulled back, shaggy waves knotted at the crown of their head. It looks like a shaggy mullet. Who the hell looks this good with a mullet? Even through the bulky layers of their winter clothes, she can tell their torso and thighs are broader, like they're intimately familiar with heavy lifting —

Their voice is deeper, too. "You're staring."

Rowen clears her throat as she buttons up her coat, sleeves pulling tight across her biceps. She wonders if Asher sees the changes in her, too — the weight she's gained that her mother never lets her forget. Double-chin, round cheeks, added padding to every part of her. Maybe Asher takes some satisfaction that the Rowen that abandoned them doesn't look the same as she did at twenty-two —

Her nose wrinkles as she swats the meek little voice in her head. She's stranded at the top of a snowy mountain on one end of a broken bridge. Does her body shape really top the list of concerns? "What are you doing up here? Are you visiting?"

Their head jerks toward the lodge. "I live here. Norling — Mrs. Norling pays me to keep the place from falling apart."

So Mrs. Norling still has a hand in this place. The elderly woman ran the family tree farm for years, hiring Rowen when she was just a college freshman. Her eyes narrow. Asher always hated Christmas festivities...strange that they, of all people, ended up taking care of this place.

And Rowen ended up ruining it, as is her curse with Asher. Her gaze darts guiltily toward what's left of the bridge. "I'm afraid some parts aren't holding up well."

When Asher follows her eyes, their mouth drops open. "What the fuck happened?! Is that what that noise was?"

As they stalk toward the wreckage, Rowen follows, wringing her bare hands. "I don't know. I was just standing on it, and then this herd of deer..."

Asher exhales slowly. "It's not...your fault." But even as they say it, their jaw tenses. They lift a chin toward her car.

"That yours?"

Defeated, she nods.

Asher's mouth twists. "At least it's better than your old clunker." They're silent for a long time, scanning the dropoff from one embankment to the other. "Is there anything you desperately need in your car?"

She considers it. There are things she could use, but nothing immediately necessary — but from the way Asher's asking, it sounds like she won't be able to get back to her car. "What about the other bridge? It used to —"

"The ground underneath it finally gave out a few years ago." Asher tilts their head toward the collapsed structure. "This is the only way in or out."

Rowen chews her lip. "If I climb back to the other side —"

A laugh bursts out of them. "There's no way you or anyone is climbing out of that ravine."

Nervously, she digs her hands into her pocket and knocks against her phone. Oh, thank god. There are a slew of missed calls from before she took her detour: *Mom. Mom. Mom.* Rowen swipes them away, but her heart sinks as her phone struggles between one bar and *No Service*. Despite her body's resistance, she dials her mother, bracing for the shrill onslaught. Blessedly or horribly, there's only a dismal click before her phone gives up trying to connect.

Asher runs a hand down their face. It sounds like they're fighting back a groan. "Didn't you check the weather before you drove up here?"

"N-no." *Stupid. God, why couldn't you...* Briskly, she rubs her hands over her cold arms. "It's never accurate on this side of the mountain anyway."

There's no arguing that. With a grunt, Asher sheds their heavy outer coat and holds it out to her. Before she can protest, they stop her. "Don't start. Just take it."

Gratefully, Rowen slips her arms into the sleeves and tries

not to sigh at the warmth of their body heat. Asher is still tense, turning their ear toward the forest as their eyes go glassy in thought. With them distracted, Rowen lets her gaze flick over them. Without the heavy coat, Asher's new physique is even more apparent. Their thermal Henley clings to their muscular pectorals. On their neck, black ink crawls out from their collar —

"A bad snowstorm's blowing in." Asher's voice makes Rowen jump, but she follows their gaze toward the forest. There are no signs of movement between the trees, but Asher watches as if they sense something. Every line of their body is rigid, like they're the one trapped on the wrong side of a snowy ravine. "No one's gonna make it up here in time to get you today. You remember the lake half a mile that way?"

Rowen tucks her hands into the depths of Asher's coat pockets. "The one we used for ice-skating?"

Asher nods. "It'll put you back on the other side of the ravine once it freezes enough to cross. You won't be able to drive in the snow, but I can arrange for someone to take you down the mountain in a few days."

"A few *days*?" Rowen's voice is small. Her mother's going to throw a fit. Rowen will never hear the end of it, the pinnacle of her failures replayed for the next five years...

But there's nothing she can do, is there? Rowen's heart flutters. She can't do anything. More importantly, her mother can't do anything. Rowen can't even call to let her know. A smile tugs at Rowen's lips, but she squashes it down. *This is nothing to be happy about. You're ruining your mother's Christmas and inconveniencing your...*

Rowen's eyes cut to Asher. Her...what, exactly? Her ex? Nothing between them was ever "official." Her winter fling? Even thinking the words makes Rowen's stomach riot. Her thoughts of Asher were hardly contained to one season, even if it was the only time they saw each other. There's a different word she saw while scrolling social media, a word that perfectly encapsulates the desire and heartache and unfinished business that linger with Asher.

Situationship.

Rowen's heart beat faster. "So until someone can get up here..."

Finally, Asher turns back to her, eyes hardened as much as their tone. "I guess you're staying with me."

Her toes curl in her wet boots, guilty and apologetic. "I'm really sorry. I didn't mean to bother you. Maybe there's somewhere else —"

"There is nowhere else." Jaw tight, Asher loops the rifle strap over their chest, swinging the gun onto their back. "This is what we're stuck with."

Three

Rowen

There is nowhere else. This is what we're stuck with.

It stings as much as the cold blowing down the hill. Rowen turns her head, blaming any watering eyes on the wind.

Asher ducks their chin, gritting their teeth as they turn toward the hill. "Come on. It's a trek."

Rowen clenches her fingers around her phone. With one final effort, she types a message to her mother and prays it sends before signal goes out again.

```
Car trouble. I'm held up for a few days.
I'm really sorry.
```

Asher's 'trek' *is* a fucking hike. Ten years ago, Rowen

walked this road multiple times a day; now, she's already growing sweaty in the jacket. Water seeps into her socks, throat growing raw from every cold breath. *Just focus. Keep your eyes up.* As soon as she lifts her gaze, she gets a perfect view of Asher's ass hugged by their hunting pants.

Her back grows sweatier. She searches for a distraction, eyes landing on the retail cabin at the base of the hill. Her stomach drops when she sees it. "It burned down?"

Asher turns back to follow her gaze. "Oh. Yeah." They keep trudging up the hill, as if they don't want to look at the wreckage. "Faulty wiring or something. It's been gone for a while."

Rowen stares wistfully at what remains of the building. It's hard to imagine this used to be a vibrant shop, filled with homemade jams, pottery, and dolls. Mrs. Norling prided herself on providing a place for the mountain community to sell their crafts. Visiting families came to the Christmas tree lodge for a fully festive experience. A cabin painted like a gingerbread house was the perfect place to buy last-minute gifts.

Now, the cabin is nothing but a charred husk, blackened walls supporting a flimsy roof that's caving in with snow. It fills her with unease, just like the abandoned buildings she passed on her way here. She zips Asher's coat to her chin, caught on another eerie feeling as she scrambles to keep up with them. "Why was that deer hanging by the bridge?"

Asher halts in the snow. Their expression is unreadable, head on a swivel as Rowen tries to meet their eyes. After a moment, Asher hikes their shoulders and continues walking. "I was dressing it after hunting."

Rowen's brows knit as she pulls her foot from a deep snow bank. That deer didn't look fresh. It looked frozen and hard, as if it had been there for weeks. But what does she know? Asher's the one who lives on this mountain, and they're prickly enough at her presence. Better not to push the issue. Their answer explains their sudden appearance...and the rifle.

"Was it acting weird when you shot it?" Rowen asks. Asher doesn't pull their gaze from the woods around them, so she clarifies. "I saw a sign on the drive up about the wildlife acting...strange. Is that why everything's abandoned?"

A twig snaps in the forest. Asher's jaw flexes as they search the woods, but there's no sign of movement. It doesn't calm Asher, and it also doesn't push them to answer her question. Instead, they keep hiking with seemingly renewed fervor. "We're almost there. Let's get inside."

Nothing pierces the chilly wall Asher keeps between the two of them. Rowen almost snorts: *Still a conversationalist, I see.* Then she clamps her lips shut, cheeks flaring with embarrassment. Where did that come from? She would never make a snarky remark like that back home to her boss or friends or, god forbid, her mother. Then again, being on this mountain always made her feel different, as if she could shed the pretense and agreeableness and just...be.

Or maybe it's because she's near Asher again. Maybe some long-forgotten pieces of herself are awakening from the proximity.

Rowen can't help but watch them as the two of them continue up the hill. Asher's a little jumpy, but more than any change to their appearance is this new sturdiness, like they're taking up every inch inside their skin. Certain. Unapologetic. *Not waiting around for you to get your shit together, that's for sure.* It makes her world tilt slightly off its axis...or maybe that's just the altitude.

When they reach the top of the hill, the lodge looks like a faded photograph, swarming Rowen with warm memories and a brand new melancholy. The two-story Bavarian cottage stands exactly where she remembers, but its red and green trim has faded. There are no pine boughs or flickering candles or wreaths, not a drop of holiday spirit to speak of. The long wall of windows shows a cold and dark interior, save for the furry creature that bounds to the front door. It's a blond Shina Inu mix, curled tail wagging when it catches sight of Asher.

Rowen gapes. "Is that yours?"

Asher stomps their snowy boots on the porch. "Unfortunately." It doesn't *look* unfortunate; it looks like Asher's trying to suppress their smile as the dog's tongue lolls happily.

"I thought you didn't like animals," Rowen teases. The Asher she knew kept their distance from people and pets alike.

With a roll of their eyes, Asher pushes open the front door. "Get stuck up here long enough, and you'll see what changes."

The thought zings through her before she quickly shakes it away. It's a silly flight of fancy. This isn't a holiday, it's an inconvenience — for her *and* Asher. Asher meant nothing by their comment, and the mountain is nothing like it used to be. She needs to remember that.

The dog bounds onto the porch, nails tapping as he jumps on Asher's legs. Once he's given Asher sufficient attention, he lowers to sniff Rowen's knees. Asher gestures between them. "This is Bard."

Rowen holds out her palm toward the animal. "Like from Dungeons & Dragons?"

Asher tugs off their gloves. "He likes to sing. I found him crooning with a broken leg a few towns over."

Bard's nose leaves a wet print on Rowen's hand before his wagging tail beats against his body. "Pretty boy," she coos, scratching gently behind his ears. Bard presses into her hand for more, the same way Asher used to when she played with their hair... She swallows the memory, giving Bard a solid pat and following Asher inside.

The interior of the cabin hasn't changed much. There's a kitchen and dining alcove to the left, opening into a cozy common area with vaulted ceilings and a massive stone fireplace. A wooden staircase leads to the second floor, where a landing wraps around its entirety. Past the railing are all eight of the guest rooms overlooking the common area.

The layout feels familiar, but everything is...empty. All the guest room doors are closed. There are no extra tables in the dining area, just the corner breakfast booth and a long expanse of open space. Only one small couch faces the fireplace, made even smaller by the huge area rug beneath it. Even the decor has been removed, leaving only a single painting of a hound chasing a stag on the far wall. It doesn't look like someone has stepped foot inside here in the last ten years, let alone that this is someone's *home*.

In the kitchen, Asher stuffs something under the sink. "You want something to drink?" They lift a steaming kettle from the stovetop. "I can make coffee or tea."

Rowen's eyes are draw straight to their fingers. Asher has tattoos there, too. She wonders where else those tattoos spread, and what they mean... Distracted, Rowen sheds her coat and nearly misses one of the hooks by the door. "Tea is fine."

Asher rifles through one of the cupboards. "Still green with lemon?"

"Yes..." Her eyes narrow. "You don't — you didn't like green tea before."

"Correct."

"Why do you have it in your pantry?" Rowen slips her wet boots and socks off. "Change of heart?"

"Nope." Asher pours water into two mugs. "I thought I'd try it again a few years ago. Still sucks." They cross the living room to hand one to her. "This teabag is probably expired, so don't get too excited."

She can't help but smile when she takes the warm mug in hand. It heats her palms and face as she lifts it to her lips, basking in the heat.

"Let it cool first," Asher calls over their shoulder, as if they have eyes in the back of their head. As if they remember how easily she used to burn her mouth. When Asher starts moving through the lodge, Rowen follows and listens. "Most things are in the same place — fire extinguisher, candles, matches..." Asher points as they go through the tour. "Electricity is iffy. I can show you the generator later. There's no cable or internet, but there's a TV over the hearth with some DVDs. Other than that..." They glance back to her, eyes following the curves of her body. Their look takes longer than it needs to — doesn't it? Rowen's fingers clench around her mug before Asher pulls their gaze away. "I'll look through the attic later and see if there are any spare clothes. In the meantime, I'll get you something warm to change into. You know where the blankets are."

Asher slips through the door behind the fireplace, into the main bedroom where Mrs. Norling used to stay. Rowen stands awkwardly near the fireplace, curling her cold toes against the rug as Asher shuffles in the other room. After a moment, they return with a handful of sweatpants, thermals, and thick socks.

"Use whatever you like." They set the folded clothes on the arm of the couch, jerking their thumb back toward the room. "Do you need to call anyone? Whoever you were on your way to see, or...?"

Rowen's mouth opens before she reconsiders. "No." Anxiety creeps up her spine. *You need to call your mother. She's waiting on you!* But the thought of her mother's screeching when Rowen explains how she ended up here, how she's spoiling her mother's holiday plans, makes Rowen shudder. Maybe she'll call later...it's not like her mother's going to worry.

Asher accepts it without further prodding, kneeling to toss some logs and kindling into the fireplace. "I called down the mountain. One of the guys in town said he'll try to get up here early on the 24th, so you can salvage your holiday."

Rowen's mouth twists. "If he can't make it until after Christmas, it's f-"

"I need you out of here by then."

It stings more than she expects. Her nails scrape the mug, making both her and Asher wince. Asher's mouth twists as if they're reconsidering their words, but they don't take them back.

"I have shit to do," they finally say, bracing one arm against the fireplace. "That's all."

When Asher crouches, the muscles in their forearms shift as they lean close to blow on the sparking embers. From this angle, Rowen can make out more of the tattoo climbing up Asher's throat. Is that...

They push up from the crackling fire, dusting their hands as they start toward the door. "Have whatever you want from the kitchen. I'll be back later tonight."

Rowen blinks the glaze from her eyes. "You're leaving?"

Asher is all business, pulling on their outer layers again. "I need to check my traps before the storm rolls in. Finish some work around the property." They zip their coat up to their neck. "You don't have any dietary restrictions, do you? Options are limited up here."

"No..." Her mind trips over itself, grasping for some way to keep them close by. "But I could come with you. If we find some clothes in the attic, maybe your work would go faster if I —"

"No."

Her body tingles, nerves fluttering in her chest. What is she doing? It feels wrong to just let them leave when they haven't addressed anything. When tension still hangs in the air, sharpening all their movements, springing to the end of her tongue...

Or maybe that's just her. Maybe Asher doesn't feel the past

clawing at them. Maybe it's better Rowen leaves it alone.

"Look…" Asher runs a hand through their hair before they turn soberly back to her. "You need to stay inside. Not just because of the storm. It's not like when we were kids up here. You saw the signs. The mountain's not a winter wonderland anymore. Without the crowds, all kinds of creatures wander up to the house, making sounds at night. The wildlife is…" Distantly, their head shakes. "Not right, like the signs say. You need to keep your distance."

A chill darts up Rowen's spine. Her eyes drift to the wall of windows behind Asher. From here, everything looks calm and quiet, a blanket of thick snow and trees swaying gently in the wind. There's no other movement, but Asher looks as stern as she's ever seen them.

"What about you?" she swallows. "You'll be out there with them."

"I know what I'm doing." A grim smile flickers on their lips before it disperses sharply. "Just stay inside. Promise me."

She twirls a loose thread inside the sleeve of her thin jacket, but Asher waits for an answer. "Ok." She drops her hand. "I promise."

With a curt nod, Asher bends to rub Bard's head. "He's got access to a covered dog run through the kitchen, so you don't have to let him out." Then Asher murmurs something to Bard, holding his face in their hands until he barks. Satisfied, Asher slips out the door without a look back.

Letter #1

I can't believe I'm starting this year without you. You'd say I did it before we met, but it's hard to remember what life was like then. I don't like to think about it. Last month, I didn't think I'd ever have to live like that again...but I was wrong.

Everything was harder before you. Does that mean things will be even harder now?

I don't want to think like that. Maybe it's naive, but I keep hoping my phone will ring, and it'll be you, and we'll say sorry and make up and stop fighting. I tried to call you, but your phone is disconnected. I don't know if it's because of me or something else. You always were switching carriers to get a better deal, but...god, I wish you'd given me your new number before you turned it off. Why wouldn't you?

I'm sorry I didn't want to tell my mom about us. It's just...you know how she is. It's hard when she's everywhere and has her hands in everything. She'll only pay my tuition if I live with her and abide by her rules, but I'm so close to being free of it. Just a few more months, remember? We could have waited a few more months...but you're right. I don't stand up for myself. I'm going to try and be better about it, ok? Even if we aren't talking, because once we start again, I want you to be proud of me. I want you to see that I could do it, and I would do it, for you. Just please call me.

I know I told you never to send anything to my mom's house, but I'm regretting it now. I called Mrs. Norling to see if she had your new number or address. She said she didn't, but she told me I could write to the tree farm, and she'd get the letters to you. I don't know how she plans to do that; you won't be back at the farm until next Christmas, if you go back at all. I can't go without hearing from you for that long.

I guess I'll keep this letter in the back of my closet with everything else of yours, until I figure out how to reach you.

Happy New Year, wherever you are,
Rowen

Four

Asher

This is just fucking perfect.

Asher doesn't look back toward the cabin, gritting their teeth at the strain in their chest. They need to get out of sight. They need to get *away*. Birds scatter from the treetops as Asher moves through the brush, head down and eyes peeled.

Pain shifts to their leg, making them curse as they brace against a boulder. Their eyes cinch shut as they will the gnawing cramp away. They can fight it off. They can subdue it. *Deep breaths...*

Carefully, they inhale through their nose, relishing the sting of cold before they realize what scent lingers in their nostrils. Minty-fresh and sharp, mixed with citrus from some fancy shampoo.

Fucking Rowen.

Just the thought of her makes their control slip, fingers curling in their gloves. What the fuck is she doing here? It's been a decade, and Asher long since resigned themself to never seeing her again. It's bad enough every inch of this mountain is drenched in memories of her. Now they have the real fucking thing standing in their living room, sitting on their couch, lying in their sheets...

No. *Fuck*. No, she's not. She's safe in the cabin, doing something innocent like playing with Bard. Bard, who Asher swears understood them when they told him to look after her. Mourning tightens Asher's throat. Now that the dog has recovered — months ago, if Asher's being truthful — it's time they take him back down the mountain. It'll be lonely as hell again, but Bard doesn't belong in this wretched place.

Neither does Rowen. Asher sucks in a breath, cool air pricking their chest. They shouldn't be thinking about it, but she has changed in the past ten years. Grown into herself. They hadn't even recognized her from behind. Her body is thick and lush, like bread rising in the oven, full-figured and mouth-watering. She's matured, as if she's lived instead of remaining trapped in Asher's memory. This older, real-life version of Rowen is impossibly more gorgeous, all her features enhanced. Bright brown puppy-dog eyes turning down at the corners, honey-brown tendrils of hair framing her face, bottom lip pouting even further...

Her makeup is still perfect, too. It always was when she came to the mountain, until she grew tired of applying it. It never took more than a few days for her to forgo it, tilting her face to the sky and letting the sun warm her bare skin.

There's always been something like that about Rowen, some part of her that couldn't be set loose anywhere else. Asher remembers her pictures from college, dressed up at some formal event or shaking hands as she accepted an award. Prim and polished in sundresses and tennis skirts, a pretty smile on her face.

But on the mountain, she let go of something: responsibilities, classes, expectations. Or maybe she found something else, some part of her that was hungry and vying to be set free. The rest of the staff called her "Wild Rowen" when she took her first drink of the season, wind whipping her hair as she took any dare that was offered.

Dares that usually ended with her making needy sounds on Asher's tongue. Craving stirs deep in their gut. Is Wild Rowen still there, buried beneath everything else? Does she have the same dark circles under her eyes? Deepend smile lines? More freckles across her nose and shoulders?

Asher's throat tightens. These are exactly the kinds of questions they shouldn't be asking. They shouldn't be wondering anything about Rowen. Clearly, she's back in her cardigan of a life, nonthreatening and unassuming. Asher's learned enough about her now in rare glimpses from social media, sitting at the public library three towns over. Rowen's done well for herself. Perfect achievements. Perfect career. Perfect string of boyfriends, all from the same mold.

Everything in Rowen's world is picturesque. No doubt getting stranded in the wilderness threw a wrench in her plans. Her arrival here means nothing. At best, it's an unfortunate mistake, and at worst...an accident meant to torture them.

I saw the gift you left for me.

Asher buries their face in their hands. *Fuck*. This is the last thing they need. They thought they'd gotten a handle on this Voice, that they'd dug a hole for it and buried it in the back of their mind.

The Voice swoops closer, as spectral as rustling leaves. **You know I'll never leave you.**

Pain pulses at Asher's temples. They brace against the rock to stay upright.

What did you hope to accomplish with your little

present? Growing pains stretch through Asher's limbs. **Poor creature strung up by its legs, gutted and rotting...**

Asher remembers the buck at the bottom of the hill. *It's a warning*, they seethe.

The Voice chuckles darkly. **A warning to whom?**

Asher exhales through their teeth. They found the stag weeks ago, its body torn to shreds as it gasped and shuddered but never died. An animal had gotten ahold of it — a few, by the looks of it. Only Asher could put the poor creature out of its misery. Only Asher can kill anything on this mountain...

At least, since this fucking Voice came along.

Asher glares into the distance. *To you. So you can see what you've done. So you'll stay the fuck away.*

Loud and demanding, the Voice expands in their head and rushes through the rest of their frame. **You know I can never leave you.**

A claw drags against the inside of Asher's ribs, making them hiss. "Stop." *God, this fucking curse...*

For a moment, the pressure subsides. The Voice is almost gentle. **Death is natural. We are not cursed, we are stuck; I can no longer oversee the balance of this place. We are weighing down one side of the scale.**

They've heard this spiel a hundred times before, but it doesn't make life on this mountain any less abysmal. Ever since they got trapped with the Voice, there's been nothing but winter here. All the flora and fauna of this place are cursed, haunted, *whatever*, trapped in a constant state of decay. It's...unnatural. Horrifying.

The mountain needs the circle of life and death, predator and prey, changing of seasons...

Asher waves the words away, but the silence in their head won't last. The Voice inhabits their body, climbing into their mind when it wants to be heard. It's another set of hands grappling for control, trying to jerk Asher into the depths so the Voice can take over.

It's been under control for months, falling dormant the last time Asher screamed and cursed it away. How foolish of them to think it might be gone for good. They've spent a decade battling it, but when Christmas Eve approaches, it always returns.

There is no privacy in Asher's thoughts. The Voice is always listening. **I return for the Wild Hunt. Would you rather I leave you to fight off the creatures alone?**

Yes, Asher grits. The Voice snorts, but Asher means it. Maybe they should let the haunted animals catch them and tear them apart. At nightfall on Christmas Eve, the beasts will hunt Asher to see how they plan to heal the curse. Like every year, Asher will have nothing to offer, and everything on this mountain will continue to decay.

The ink in Asher's skin burns, an electric fence trying to keep the Voice pinned inside. **I think you may have something to offer this year...**

A sickly feeling curdles in Asher's stomach. In the hour since Rowen arrived, the Voice feels more awake, as if it recognizes her. Senses her. *Smells* her.

She's as much mine as she is yours.

Heat strikes in Asher's stomach, flint against steely resolve...but their control slips. They allow themself the weakness, giving into the images the Voice paints in Asher's mind: Rowen's brown eyes wide, her body splayed beneath them, fingers curled in their shirt as she gasps —

Asher douses the visions, digging their nails against the inside of their gloves. *She's neither of ours. She has nothing to do with this.* They strain to their feet, taking another stilted step away from the cabin.

The Voice curls around the top of their spine, as lazy as a trail of smoke. **She hungers the same as we do.** The inside of Asher's ear grows warm as the Voice morphs into something more tantalizing. **Let me take a bite; I'll tell you how she tastes.**

A moan stifles behind Asher's lips. *No. Fuck!* Temptation coils in their stomach. *We are not anything. We are not the same. Stay the fuck away from her.*

What if we need her? What if the mountain needs her?

Fuck this Voice and its fucking riddles. Asher grits their teeth, starting toward deeper woods. As they kick through a drift of snow, a group of chipmunks scatter. Every creature in this godforsaken forest runs from Asher, until the one night a year they get to chase. *I've told you a thousand times, I don't know what you want. What the "mountain" wants.*

I've told you the way.

It plays on repeat in Asher's mind, the same impossible words that have haunted them for years.

This place will decay until magic returns to the mountain. Until our paths converge. Until you let the hound consume your heart.

It means nothing, just another slew of nonsense that makes Asher more frustrated with each passing day. As if they haven't tried everything they can think of. As if Norling didn't try everything she could while she was here. The two of them spent years visiting every mystical shop in this state, researching the mountain and assembling spells from every book they could find. They followed every trail in the forest twice over, lingering at crossroads and creating new ones. Asher even considered serving their heart to Bard for dinner, but that seemed traumatic for both of them.

It's been ten years of this riddle, and it never leads to anything. *You don't even know what the words mean.* Asher picks up speed, sliding down the snowy slope. *You just repeat them to make yourself feel better.*

I have a thought.

The heavy coldness of the Voice makes Asher halt, gripping a tree to keep from sliding. They don't like the way the Voice sounds, the way it waits for Asher to question it. The way it wants Asher to hear and engage. *What thought?*

The hound...it could be me.

Asher huffs a laugh. *You don't look like a dog.*

But a wolfish tail sways lazily in their mind. It's true this Voice takes a shape unlike any other, morphing over the years to become something...carnivorous. What once resembled an animal of prey has begun to feel predatory. Blood-thirsty.

A set of sharpened teeth flash in Asher's mind, stretching into a smile as the Voice speaks. **I'm close enough to a hound. And this woman...*Rowen*.** At her name, Asher's stomach clenches. The claw inside them drags back up along their ribs, plinking like a xylophone. **I feel her presence in your chest, right...here.**

The claw presses out against Asher's skin, drawing an X above their heart.

Asher's jaw clicks. They can't keep a secret from this *thing* inhabiting their body. The Voice felt the painful twist in Asher's chest as soon as they recognized Rowen...but it takes a moment for Asher to realize what the Voice means.

Cold sweat breaks along their body. *Rowen is not the 'heart' of your fucking prophecy. You're not going to kill her. You're not going to — fucking eat her!*

Even thinking it sounds ludicrous, but the Voice taps Asher's sternum. **Perhaps the magic does not require her death. Maybe I need only a limb...a drop of blood...** Asher's mouth tastes coppery as the Voice licks its lips, long and slow. **A taste of her perfect cunt.**

Arousal brands in Asher's stomach as their fist clenches and snaps the branch in their hand. *Rowen is not a part of this,* they repeat. *You're not getting close to her.*

Foolish mortal: this vessel belongs to both of us.

The Voice surges like a wave, pressing out against every inch of Asher's body. ***You* cannot get close to her without *me*.**

There's no stopping the Voice now. Its fury pounds inside of Asher, water against rocks at the bottom of a fall, sucking Asher deeper every time they come up for air. Their arms stretch past the sleeves of their coat, knees trembling as the joints fight to bend backwards.

Asher sinks into the snow, trying to cling to the tree root beside them. Gritting their teeth, they strip off their clothing, groaning as familiar pain rips through their body. It's been so long since they lost control. Since the Voice forced its way out. Their blood rushes hot, blurring out the pain of snow against their bare skin.

An agonizing crack breaks across their forehead, as if their skull is splitting in two. They have to get further from the cabin. They can't risk the beast inside them getting near Rowen. If Asher can pull themself away long enough to exhaust the Voice...

Stumbling, they pull themself onto four legs and stagger down the hill. There's only one refrain in their head: *Away. Away. Away.* Then their thoughts are lost as the Voice grows as loud as their thundering pulse.

The more you fight, the worse it gets.

Five

Rowen

The lodge feels like the inside of a snow globe.

A snow globe in the hands of a child. The gray clouds have finally made good on their threat, pouring snowflakes between evergreens as the snowdrifts grow higher. Wind rattles the window panes, making Rowen shiver as she peers out into the darkness.

Inside the lodge, everything is quiet. Snow muffles the storm as Bard dozes on the living room rug. Even the fire gives hushed pops and cracks as Rowen wraps a blanket tighter around her shoulders. As daylight fades, her shadow grows darker against the windows, the fire behind her the brightest source of light.

Back when this was a functioning farm, this wall of

windows was a selling point, giving uninterrupted views of the mountain. At nightfall, though, Rowen can only make out a rough outline of trees through the storm. There's nothing scenic about it; she can't see anything.

The lodge is a glowing beacon atop the abandoned mountain, and it feels like *Rowen's* the view.

She shudders, hiking her shoulders as she turns away. It's a silly thought. If there were anyone else on this mountain, she wouldn't be stuck trying to entertain herself with Asher's slim selection. After a haphazardly-assembled lunch, she watched a few movies, but they left something to be desired. None of the films Rowen could find had the slightest inkling of Christmas coziness. What happened to the holiday classics that used to line these shelves? Or even the worn puzzles and games? When Rowen opened the familiar armoire, it was hollow and empty, much like the rest of the cabin.

That was hours ago, and Asher still hasn't returned. Worry gnaws at her as she makes her way back onto the couch and tucks her feet beneath her. Bard twitches in his sleep. It's been so long since Asher left, she's gotten past the awkwardness of being alone in their house. Her eyes flick to the main bedroom, where Asher must sleep now.

Maybe that's the only part of this lodge that has any sign of life in it. She could take a look inside, get a glimpse of what Asher's like now. Do they still keep a water bottle beside their bed? Do they use the same quilt Rowen spent so many nights under? Do they —

Something mechanical whirs as all the lights flick off. Rowen and Bard's heads shoot straight up.

Of course: the power's gone out. Asher did say it was iffy.

Rowen shifts nervously at the sudden silence, but Bard just rests back on the carpet. Good. That's good. This must be pretty common if the dog isn't freaking out. If Bard's not worried, she doesn't need to be, either.

At least the fire still sheds plenty of light, even if the room feels colder now. Rowen tucks her hands into the sleeves of her borrowed sweatshirt. Truthfully, it was a relief to get out of her stuffy clothes. She's always been a "big shirt, tiny shorts" kind of girl, and the selection Asher left is oversized, even for her. A decade ago, that wouldn't have been the case, but Asher has...grown.

The word stirs sinfully in Rowen's stomach. She pushes the blanket aside — so much for feeling colder. But she can't think about Asher like that. Things are awkward enough without her growing hot at the thought of how different they are. *Some* things haven't changed at all, like Asher's impulsive need to get as far from her as possible. Hell, they went out into a blizzard rather than spend a few hours with her in their own home.

The thought jabs into her chest. Things really are as tense as she always imagined they'd be. In the years since they last spoke, she wondered if she was overthinking. Maybe Asher wouldn't have any reaction to her. Maybe they wouldn't even remember her — but those were pipe dreams. This tension isn't about their last fight. In the grand scheme of things, it was small...but the years between them aren't. All those unspoken words and feelings locked inside and compounded into silence, this thing between them left unfinished and unacknowledged.

Sweat pricks the back of her neck. She needs to take her mind off it, but with no electricity...her eyes rove the walls and chimney, glazing over brick and wood. There is truly nothing in this cabin. The bare minimum pieces of furniture are gathered in the center of the room like an island. Around it is a sea of nothingness, much like the cabin on the mountain.

Much like its caretaker.

Guilt tightens Rowen's throat. Asher wasn't always like that. Or, they *were*, but she managed to fashion a bridge and make her shaky way across it...but that was years ago. She rests her head back against the couch. Maybe she is overthinking. Maybe the cabin isn't as vacant as she thinks. Maybe it's her knowledge of how bright and magical this place used to be that shines a glaring spotlight on how much it lacks.

Wind whistles against the lodge as Rowen tries to peer through the snow for any sign of movement. There's nothing. A nervous pit forms in her stomach, but she presses it down. Asher knows what they're doing. They do this on their own every day, and they're fine. They must be doing something right.

But surely they don't need *that* much meat. Asher can't need half a day to check traps for only themself and Bard, especially judging by the food stores in the kitchen. Everything is so...*bland,* filled more like a survivalist bunker than someone's pantry. Asher isn't eating for pleasure — no holiday treats, only necessary carbs and protein. Back when they worked together at this lodge, she couldn't make a batch of cookies or cider without Asher sneaking a taste. What happened to that?

Something scurries along the roof, claws scrambling before they disappear. Bard lifts his head, ears perking as Rowen tries to soothe herself. It's just a squirrel or a raccoon...but she can't shake the memory of the hole in the staff closet ceiling where smaller creatures could get in. God, wouldn't that be perfect? Some critter darting through the cabin with only Rowen and Bard to capture it in the dark. Surely Asher patched the hole by now...but when the sounds of tiny claws come again, Rowen sets her feet on the ground. Better safe than sorry. It's not like she'll be able to think about anything else until she checks, and there's nothing else to do.

Lighting a candle from the end table, she moves toward the stairway, but something stops her. In the past, the lodge was full of life and light, families gathered for stories and laughter and games. Rowen never considered this place could be eerie, but now, there's only absence. Darkness. Silence. The light from the fire just reaches the second-story railing, but beyond it, the closed rooms along the balcony are black holes

Maybe something is here. Watching. Waiting for you.

Wax drips onto her finger, making her squeak as she readjusts her grip. Her face heats with pain and embarrassment. No one saw that, because no one is watching her. No one is *here.*

Determined, she lifts her chin and takes her first step up the stairs. Wind shrieks against the cabin, but Bard doesn't move from the rug. *That's a good sign*, she tells herself. *He's used to this, like a pilot with turbulence. There's nothing to worry about...*

Aside from Asher's absence. God, where are they? Rowen glances toward the wall of windows again, but she can't make out anything from this distance, only a reflection of the living room. It's so dark outside...

The fire pops. She grits her teeth to keep from jumping. *Christ, calm down. You've spent how many hours in this lodge over the years? It isn't scary. It's a Christmas paradise.* Yet her body stays rigid, gaze darting over her shoulder as she lingers on the first step.

Enough. She *has* to walk through the second story now, to set her mind at ease and show herself how silly she's being. Once she takes a look upstairs, she'll get a better view of the mountain and prove there's nothing lurking in the shadows, and she can get back to boredom.

Beneath her, the stairs creak. At least that sound is recognizable. She eases her weight in a familiar pattern — the right side of the middle step, the center of the next two, the far left of the last...

As she ascends, the creaking stops. She and the stairs remember each other; that hasn't changed.

At least something about this mountain hasn't.

Once Rowen steps onto the second-floor landing, she's engulfed in shadows. From up here, the living room looks even brighter...which makes everything around her darker. Guest rooms line the walkway on all four sides, doors shut tight as far as Rowen can see. The railing wraps around the entire landing, like a balcony above the living room.

There's no sign of anything, critter or otherwise.

Her first step is hesitant, letting the wood settle beneath her before she sets her full weight on it. She takes one solid step, then another, until she's tip-toeing past the doors with only a slight trip in her pulse.

See? She forces herself to exhale. *There's no need to sneak around. Nothing else is here.*

To prove it, she presses her ear against the door in the far corner of the landing. No sound at all. Palm slick, she wipes it on her shirt before she twists open the knob. The door swings back into darkness, lit only by the glow of her candle. Despite the shadows, this room is comforting, slowing the thrum of her heart. The staff closet looks much the way she remembers, shelving units along the wall covered in folded linens and candles. She runs a finger through dust on one shelf at eye level. Mrs. Norling wouldn't have let that fly. A smile flickers across Rowen's mouth. At least Mrs. Norling didn't know about the loose floorboard under the window, where the staff hid mini liquor bottles to spike their drinks on hot cocoa nights.

Nostalgia gets the better of her. She takes a step inside, disturbing motes of dust on the floor. Her chest twinges. Everything is in the same place, as if one of the other staffers might sneak in giggling at any moment. It's like a time capsule, a shot of the inside of Rowen's head, her memories undisturbed for years and covered in dust. Looking at this room now feels like she's watching the final grains of sand slipping through an hourglass.

The space is suddenly stifling. She sets her candle on an empty shelf and moves toward the window, using her sleeve to wipe away the fog. There's more to see from up here, but not much. The forest of evergreens and bare trees slope down the hill, lining the drive she'd climbed this morning.

Maybe she can catch sight of Asher from up here. She lifts on her toes as if that might reveal them, but the forest is thick and dark. Nothing peeks through the trees. No headlamp. No flashlight. No movement at all.

Wrinkling her nose, she leans closer, hissing when her skin touches the frigid glass. Most of the trees in the forest are massive, undisturbed for years, but there's one shorter than the others. Between two twisted trunks, this smaller tree's branches stretch horizontally. They're oddly symmetrical, almost like...

Antlers.

Fog seeps across the glass. Rowen smears it away again and searches for the smaller tree. It's hard to find her place in the dark, especially through swirling snow, but she finally lands on the mysterious shadow again.

It still looks like antlers. Her eyes narrow. Could it be another buck? But if the creature is alive, it's eerily still, almost as if it's a part of the forest. She can't make out any details through the storm, but its face appears lighter than the tree around it, closer to the color of the snow.

If she didn't know any better, she'd think its head was...a skull.

The shadow blurs when the glass fogs again. Her heart lodges in her throat, bare fingers smearing against the glass as she holds her breath to keep it from fogging.

Her gaze darts over the treeline, stumbling back to the place between the twisted trees. Even when she squints, she can't make out the shadow anymore. There is no tree. No antlers. Nothing between the two bending trunks.

The creature must have moved. She swallows, breath still held tight in her lungs. That makes sense. A deer moving through the forest? That's normal. That's natural.

But a *skeletal* deer isn't.

Rowen

Rowen steps back from the window. There has to be a reason for whatever she thought she saw. It was a trick of the light, made worse by the storm raging.

God, where the hell is Asher?

Anxiety peaks in Rowen's chest as she grabs the candle and leaves the room behind. At least the light from the fireplace is visible back on the landing. She basks in what brightness she can get, taking slow breaths as she sets the candle on the railing. Has she gotten cabin fever already? That must be why she's so jumpy. Now that she's out of the confined closet, it's easy to tell herself she didn't see anything at all. The fireplace below runs the creepy thoughts out of her mind.

For the most part, at least. Shadows still skirt along the

walls, firelight casting shapes across the only portrait in the living room. Its background is lush and green, but the flutter of the fire makes it look as if it's moving. Rowen leans against the railing, trying to make out the shapes through the darkness. It looks the same as the first time she saw it: a deer leaping through the snow in a tranquil forest, reminiscent of this very mountain...but something's off about it. Her eyes narrow. Has the picture...changed?

It's impossible. Even thinking the question is ludicrous, but she scans the details to reassure herself. There's the deer, and the snow, and the hound — yes, there it is, a honey-brown creature leaping after the stag.

Beneath it, a large splotch of red stands out against the snowy ground. Rowen's fingers curl around the railing as she leans further, trying to see past the shadows wobbling along the bottom of the frame. Red paint drips from the deer's stomach, leaving a trail as it runs. Only now does she see the deer's eyes wide with fear, its mouth open in a silent scream. The dog isn't just chasing the deer. As the shadows move again, she sees the dog's teeth clamping around the deer's haunch.

Her stomach roils. She pushes back, trying to steady the rapid pace of her heart. She'd only given the portrait a cursory glance before. It's hard to see past the shadows now, constantly shifting and changing to make the paint look like it's moving. Maybe Rowen just missed something before. Maybe the dog was always that close, its teeth always digging into the deer —

There's movement beside her. Rowen fights down a scream before she realizes she's looking at the window just outside the closet door. Fumbling closer, she wipes the fog away and presses up against the glass. From the trees, a shadow staggers toward the lodge, a solitary speck among the white of the ground. The shadow's feet dig a trench through the snow. Rowen tries to clear the fog again, but the wind outside blurs everything. Even cupping her hand over her eyes, the shadow's shape is indecipherable. It's not quite human, not quite animal, not quite —

A howl rips through the house.

Rowen scrambles back, stumbling into the railing and sending her candle plummeting to the first floor. It lands wick-first, stuttering out against the rug...and Bard is nowhere to be seen.

The howl comes again. Rowen leans over the railing to see into the kitchen where Bard sits beneath a window, head tilting back mournfully as he cries...

Something answers him. One animal voice, then another, until an entire chorus carries on the wind. The calls scatter into yips and barks, growing louder as they echo off of rocks and trees.

Below her, the first-story windows rattle. She falls to her knees, trying to catch sight of anything outside. There's nothing — only the wind. Only the snow. When Bard howls again, she pulls herself to her feet and stumbles down the stairs.

Back on the first floor, she's even more exposed, socked feet slipping against the wood. Her head whips toward every inch of glass. Only the glowing fireplace reflects back at her, outlining her silhouette as she scurries across the room.

A long-forgotten instinct screams at her, hair lifting on her neck. *Something's watching. It's there, out the window. It moved just before you turned your head...*

In the kitchen, she reaches down to pet between Bard's ears, praying the motion soothes her as much as him. "Are you singing to someone out there?"

Bard keeps his eyes sharpened out the window. Her pitiful laugh dies in her throat.

From this vantage point, she can make out the hillside she climbed earlier today. A quarter mile down is her car and the covered bridge clinging to the bank...but at the top of the hill is something else. Something that moves.

It staggers through the snow toward the cabin. It's a massive beast, but its movements aren't right. They're lumbering and jilted, like it's half-dragging its body behind it. Rowen blinks to clear her eyes. That can't be what she's seeing. It's a trick of the storm and her nervous mind— but then another shape appears, then another, all prowling toward the lodge.

The front door slams open. She screams as Bard's toenails scrabble on the floor. A heavy figure thuds inside, forcing the door shut against the wind before it claws at its head. "Fuck's sake, Rowen, it's *me*!"

Only once she can breathe does she recognize Asher's voice and very human body. There's no sign of the skeletal deer or lumbering creatures she thought she saw.

Bard bounds happily toward Asher, jumping at their legs as Rowen presses a hand to her throat. "I thought..." Her heart pounds. She tries to swallow around it. "There's something coming over the hill. Something big."

With a grim expression, Asher tugs off their beanie and moves toward the window. Rowen peers around them, trembling at the memory — but even through the storm, she can see there's nothing. No lurking figures. No echoing howls.

She exhales the breath she'd kept trapped in her lungs. Asher moves back to the entryway, tugging off the rest of their outwear. "I told you, there are all kinds of animals out there. Nothing's gonna bother you in here." When they flick the lightswitch to the living room, nothing happens. "No wonder you were wound-up," they grumble. "Must be a fallen tree. I'll look for it tomorrow."

Asher loads more wood into the fire. Rowen leans against the arm of the couch, adrenaline flagging. She *was* scaring herself. There's nothing skulking around outside, nothing except Asher after leaving her for hours by herself. "Those traps must be huge if they took that long."

Dusting off their hands, Asher leaves the blazing fire behind with a shrug. "You know shit on the mountain. It never goes smoothly."

She watches them kick off their boots. "So where is it?"

Asher lifts a brow.

"The meat," she reminds them, rising and moving toward the kitchen. "From the traps. Where is it?"

"Oh." Asher presses a hand against the wall for balance. "I put it in the ice house already." Their thermal shirt rides up, exposing the muscled indentations of their lower back.

Rowen's gaze clings to that strip of skin. "You didn't have to go through all that trouble..." Her voice is breathy. What is she talking about? Oh, right. "I'm not expecting five-course meals or anything. I'll only be here for a few days."

Guilt gnaws at her, even if it's true. Asher's return to the cabin brings a return of tension. Her body feels sweaty and chilly at once, and she's suddenly aware of how alone they are. There's all this space on the mountain, all this space inside the lodge, but they're sharing the same ten feet.

Asher rests their foot back on the ground, avoiding her gaze. "It's no big deal. I would have done it anyway." Firelight glows up their throat, painting them warm and golden in the dark. The only skin she can see is their face and neck, her eyes drawn to the way their throat bobs when they look at her. She shivers, folding her arms across her chest before she remembers she's wearing their clothes.

Asher seems to recall it at the same time, eyes clinging to the fabric draped over her body. Before she can thank them for the clothing, Asher moves past her into the kitchen. Static zaps between their shoulders, making Rowen gasp as Asher reaches instinctively for her. Their fingers curl around the backs of her elbows. Even through the fabric, she can tell their hands are different. Thicker. Calloused. Sturdier.

Their mouth hangs open, words forgotten in their mouth as their eyes dip to hers. She sucks in a slow breath, lips parting, as if anything too sudden will shock her again. Asher's hands leave a warm place on her skin.

"Sorry," they finally manage, dropping their hands to their side.

She tries to remember how to breathe. Her fingers flit toward her elbows, but she forces them down as Asher moves toward the stove.

"I'm sure you're hungry," they call over their shoulder, as if speaking too softly is dangerous. As if it will get them into trouble...or maybe that's Rowen's wishful thinking. With a careful hand, Asher turns on the gas stove and sends a circle of blue flame flaring to life. Rowen wonders if it's half as hot as she feels, but she smothers the thought when Asher glances back at her. "How about that five-course meal you aren't expecting?"

Seven

Asher

Cooking is...different with another person in the kitchen. Bard searches for dropped food underfoot, which only makes things that much more cramped. Asher mutters apologies and tries to avoid bumping into Rowen, but the two of them can't stay out of each other's way.

Asher clenches their teeth. "Why don't you sit down, Rowen? You're a guest." That's not the only reason they want her out of their space, but it'll suffice. Her sitting and watching has to be better than knocking into each other in the dark. In such a short time, Asher's body is already so aware of hers, prickling every time the two of them get close.

Rowen almost heeds the suggestion, straying to the edge of the island with a wistful look. Her mouth is clamped in that way that means she wants to say something, but she doesn't want to rock the boat...classic Rowen. But instead of taking a seat, her brows knit, a flash of that wild something in her eyes. "I've been sitting all day. Waiting for *you*." The word is almost sharp. Asher can't help but be a little impressed before Rowen backs into gentleness again. "At least let me prep something. I can chop."

Her helpfulness is stubborn, if nothing else. Asher smiles despite themself, setting a cutting board and knife on the opposite side of the island. "Be careful with it in the dark. Here..." Rummaging through one of the cabinets, they retrieve a headlamp and hold it out to her.

She blinks. "I think I can manage with the candles."

Asher doesn't hesitate to wrap the lamp strap around her head, ignoring the soft feel of her hair. "I'm not having you chop off a finger while we're snowed in." Asher clicks the lamp on and raps her head. "Use the lamp."

Bright light obscures her face. Asher tries to make out the details of her expression before they realize they're staring. Once the light bobs in a nod, Asher turns back to the pot on the stove.

With their back to Rowen, they can finally breathe. Thank god she stopped asking questions. She doesn't need to know that Asher has no traps, and that any hunting here would only produce rotting corpses. There's plenty of meat in the shed from Asher's trips away from the mountain, and the Voice inside them is subdued...for now. It took hours longer than expected to let the Voice run wild and exhaust itself, but Asher couldn't risk returning to the cabin any earlier. Not when the Voice pushed its way out of Asher's body, out of their control and salivating over thoughts of Rowen.

Asher's stomach twists at the carnal memories. They need to focus on something else, their hands feeling for the spice cabinet. Cayenne, paprika, cumin...Asher brings them all down to the counter and sifts through them. They sprinkle in spices, giving the pot a taste before they pour in some beer to complement the meat.

When Rowen brings the chopped vegetables to them, she lingers over their shoulder and lifts her nose to the scent. Asher doesn't turn to look at her. It would only invite conversation, and Asher's been prolonging that as much as possible. Still, the silence is weirdly comfortable. Easy. *Too* easy, because Asher almost forgets this space between them is supposed to be awkward. It's *supposed* to be fraught. There's been a decade of time and space and life since the last time they spoke, yet this moment is...companionable.

Tension returns to their shoulders. They can't allow it to remain that way.

Once the chili has simmered, Rowen insists on setting the breakfast nook table. "I still remember how to do it." A smile flutters on her face as she folds dish towels in place of napkins, angling the silverware just so.

Asher ladles the food into two bowls and carries them to the large, curved booth. "What do you want to drink?"

"Beer's fine."

Asher grabs two bottles, but as they return to the table, they hesitate. They hadn't thought about how dangerous this would be. This nook is the only furniture left in the dining room, built into the curved wall. Either Rowen and Asher sit on opposite sides of the large table...or they eat right next to each other.

Both options are awkward and uncomfortable, but Rowen has already scooted further into the booth. Cautiously, she watches them and waits. After a long moment, Asher lights the candle on the table and sinks down next to her.

Their throat feels tight. If they shift their leg just slightly, it would touch her. One wrong move, and their elbows will brush. Asher swallows, keeping their eyes honed on their bowl as they eat in silence. In their periphery, Rowen does the same, ducking her head as she chews. Her brows knit curiously as she takes another bite.

What is she thinking? Asher wants to look at her, to see her expression, but the two of them are too damn close.

From the floor, Bard watches her just as intently, as if he's waiting for her response too. She doesn't speak.

Finally, Asher can't take it anymore, clearing their throat gruffly. "Sorry the five courses had to be condensed to one meal."

Rowen dabs her napkin against her mouth. "No, it's...good." Surprise laces her tone. "*Really* good."

Asher scoffs.

"I didn't mean —" Even in the dark, Rowen's cheeks flood with color. "You used to hate cooking. I didn't expect you to be so...capable." Her voice lowers as if she's speaking to herself. "I mean, you got out of kitchen duty for a whole season because you set a dish towel on fire."

Shit, they'd forgotten about that. It pries their mouth into a grin. In truth, they usually don't put much effort into their meals. Food is fuel, a way to keep their body warm for a day of work. But with Rowen here...they'd be lying if they said they didn't care if she was impressed, or at least pleased, with what they made her. Back in the day, Rowen was always the one feeding Asher, filling their mug or sharing what she baked or preparing a midnight snack as they sat next to her on the counter.

Maybe they wanted to take care of her for once.

The thought burns, a warm but lasting reminder of what Asher shouldn't touch. They dip their spoon into their bowl. "A lot can change in ten years."

Silence hangs over them like icicles forming on the roof of the lodge. Memories drip to a dangerous point, threatening to break off and impale them or shatter to the ground.

Asher sets their jaw, pressing back against the booth. Good: this conversation should be weird. It should be tense and awkward after the way they left things. This is not a holiday; it's a weird situation that came at a terrible time, and Asher cannot — *will not* — enjoy it. No matter how different this silence is than the silence of living alone, a silence that Asher has gotten very used to.

Rowen folds her hands in her lap. "So...what were your plans for the holiday? Before I interrupted."

She can never let them just stew in their misery. Asher shrugs. "Same as every other day: work. Eat. Sleep. Repeat."

Rowen manages not to drop her spoon. "You're not doing — anything? Not visiting anyone? Not hanging decorations?"

Asher hunches defensively over their bowl. "You know I don't like Christmas."

"Yeah, but — you're *here*." She gestures weakly toward the lodge before she realizes her point falls flat. This is not the cabin either of them remember. Whatever "Christmas spirit" it once held has been packed away in boxes or wore away with time. She scrambles for something else. "You don't do anything with Mrs. Norling?"

Asher clears their throat. "She doesn't come around anymore. Old age, illness, you know."

"You don't visit her?"

Regret swells in Asher's chest. How can they answer that? For years, Norling was the only person Asher saw, the only one who knew what they'd become, the only one who was still here. *I'm so sorry, sweetheart*. Norling reached for Asher, but they couldn't bear the touch. *I should never have let this happen. I didn't think any of it was real. I didn't know it could do this...*

It still stings, remembering her apologies when Asher was to blame. They ruined her farm and the forest and the mountain. Now, her mind is fading in the nursing home. When Asher goes to see her, she doesn't remember. She doesn't recognize that Asher cursed the mountain and destroyed her last good years. Somewhere deep, her final memories of this place are of her beloved tree farm rotting away.

That makes Asher the guiltiest of all.

"I don't leave the mountain unless I have to," they finally rasp. "Norling's just holding onto this place for the memories, and she doesn't even have those now." Their eyes flit to Rowen. "She spent all that time waiting for something that's never coming back."

Rowen's gaze drops like a kicked puppy. On the floor, Bard looks similarly wounded, as if he somehow understands what they're saying. The candle flutters on the table, the only thing in the room that moves as they both stiffen into silence again.

Asher

Bard whines and paws at Asher's foot, as if he senses the chill in Asher's temperament. Begrudgingly, Asher tries to clip the thorns from their mood. They should be civil. Show some manners. It's the only thing that's going to make the next few days bearable, and a change of topic would be more than welcome.

"What were your plans before you got stuck here?" Asher grumbles.

Rowen's spoon scrapes her bowl, making her wince. Delicately, she sets the utensil aside and injects some false cheer into her voice. "I'm actually moving back in with my mom for a little while."

Asher's brows jump. It may have been a decade, but they

remember that hike in Rowen's voice. It's the one she always uses when she speaks about her mother, pitching higher in an attempt at excitement. Asher blows steam from their spoonful of chili. "And how's that going?"

Rowen's smile twitches. "Fine. Good."

"You're full of shit."

Fuck. They dig their heels into the ground. They didn't mean to let the words slip out. They hadn't meant to say anything, but it was almost insulting watching Rowen lie like that. As if Asher doesn't know her practiced smile from her real one. As if Asher forgot how Rowen's eyes grew wet with tears every time she got off the phone with her mother.

They open their mouth to apologize, but a smile stirs on Rowen's lips. "Very kind of you to say."

Asher's mouth itches to grin. "Am I wrong?"

She leans into the table, propping her chin in her hand and stirring her spoon. "If you knew me less, I'd be a better liar, so whose fault is that?"

With a laugh, Asher reaches for their drink, but a sobering thought surfaces. Their hand closes around the bottle, inspecting the label so they can look somewhere besides Rowen. "And your mom, she still doesn't know you're...not straight?"

It's the mildest way Asher can put it, but Rowen still winces. "No." Rowen's eyes jerk up, cheeks reddening. "I've tried to tell her, but she..." A heavy breath escapes her. "She doesn't hear it. It's like I'm not even talking..."

A different thought settles into Rowen's mind. Her expression shifts into a look Asher remembers, a mix of worry and sympathy that they can't stand. Rowen realizes it at the same time, her gaze dropping back to her bowl, but it's too late; Asher's already seen it.

They brace themself. Better get it out in the open, so they can set the record straight. They don't need her silent pity.

"Whatever it is, just say it."

Despite Asher's gruffness, Rowen's voice is gentle. "What about *your* parents?"

Of course. Asher swallows too much beer, but they refuse to cough, sitting with the ache until they speak plainly. "We don't talk anymore."

"You cut them off?" Rowen sets her spoon down. "Officially?"

"It was mutual." A bitter smile crawls up Asher's face. "They couldn't pronounce my name, for some reason." They keep smiling, not unlike the phony one Rowen wore moments before — but where her facade is overly cheery, Asher's is a centimeter away from snarling. Both their smiles are masks all the same, keeping anyone from prying to see what's underneath.

It doesn't matter anyway. Asher's parents are old news, yet something sickly and weak opens its mouth inside them. They hate this part of themself, the part that's hungry and empty, always hoping to be filled instead of left echoing.

How could you do this to us? To yourself? It's not right. It's not natural. You've ruined my baby...

"I'm sorry, Asher."

Their name in Rowen's mouth brings them out of the pit. Candlelight flutters on her cheeks. It's so rare Asher gets to hear their name spoken aloud, especially from someone who knew them before. It's proof that it's possible to see them as they are, like they're the same and different than they were. Like they're real.

Asher's eyes prick, but they stuff that emotion into the bottomless pit. "Doesn't matter. Not like I'm missing out."

Rowen's fingernails *tink* against her bottle. "They are, though. And that's their fault."

Asher has told themself the same for years, but when there's no one to confirm it, they can't help wondering if their parents are right and Asher is the one causing all the damage. It wouldn't be the first time. But hearing the assurance from someone else is oddly comforting.

The gaping pit in their stomach shrinks slightly.

They run a hand back through their hair, too exposed under her gaze. "Look, we don't have to get into old shit. This is just for a few days. We can just be cordial. Try to make the most of it." Their mouth tightens over the words. "Then you go back to your life, and I go back to mine."

It's the least painful option, but Asher doesn't miss the flicker in Rowen's eyes. They can't let themself wonder at what it means. This is what has to happen.

Rowen nods numbly.

Good. Asher searches for something appropriate to say, something...host-like. "You can stay in the main bedroom while you're here — the one behind the fireplace. It's the only mattress left that wasn't eaten by moths."

"Then where are you staying?"

They tilt their head toward the living room. "The couch is fine."

"I can't take your bed," Rowen splutters. "I'm not even supposed to be here!"

"Rowen." Their voice is stern and even, brooking no arguments. Rowen's mouth clamps shut, knees knocking together beneath the table. Their eyes narrow curiously. "You sleep in the bed. I'll be fine."

When her gaze skims Asher's shoulders, they're suddenly aware of their body, their chest and arms and neck. Rowen's lips make a sound when they part, but that's all that comes out until she clears her throat. "You seem too...broad to be comfortable on the couch."

It shouldn't make Asher smug, their tongue pressing against a canine tooth before they lift the bottle again. "Thanks for noticing."

Rowen's eyes go glassy when she shifts in her seat, honed on where their mouth connects to the bottle. Asher takes their time swallowing. Rowen doesn't pull her eyes away. "Must work wonders on all the stranded travelers that end up here."

She brushes hair off her shoulder, pretending there's no curiosity in her tone. Asher knows better than that. Her words aren't a statement, they're a question, and not an innocent one either.

Asher's fingers drum against the table. They could ignore it and let the moment pass. That's what they *should* do. That's how they should treat the guest in their home, but something in that gaping pit wakes up. It churns and boils at the sight of Rowen's tongue tracing her lips.

Asher lets the quiet linger before they set their bottle back on the table. "If you want to know who I'm fucking, just ask."

Goddammit, did they not just agree to be cordial?

Blood rushes into Rowen's cheeks. Her arms tense beneath the table, and Asher wonders if she's digging her nails into her thigh the way she used to dig them into Asher's back. *Fuck*, they shouldn't let their mind go there...but Rowen meets their gaze, like she needs the answer more than she needs her dignity. "Who are you — fucking?"

The curse is breathless, her eyelashes fluttering. Little miss perfect probably hasn't said a foul word since the last time the two of them spoke.

Asher tilts their head, reveling in her fragment of rebellion. They can't let her off the hook that easily. "No one comes up here, Rowen." Their fingers drag lazily along the bottleneck. "You'd have to be pretty silly to do a thing like that."

She squirms as she watches their hand. "Never?" Her voice is tight. "In the last ten years, no one ever...came up here?"

That's not what she really wants to know. Asher can hear the real question as clearly as if she'd spoken it.

Has there been anyone else?

Jealousy sinks its teeth into Asher. They know the answer *she* would give. It's been splashed across her social media time and again, some man in a tailored suit thrilled to have Rowen on his arm.

Should it hurt more or less that the men look nothing like Asher?

They lean back in their seat. Rowen's gaze follows the motion, drilling temptation into Asher like a woodpecker. There's no one else on this mountain. There's nothing but snow and this lodge and the two of them under the same roof, circling back into familiar orbit. If they let that pull them into each other's paths...

But that thought sinks like a rock to the bottom of a lake. Nothing can happen between them, not with what Asher is now. Not with the Voice thumbing through their memories like they're a fucking card catalog.

Asher isn't made for connections or relationships or whatever the fuck this is. Asher suffers this mountain on their own. It's their fault they're here, and that's what prevents Asher from bringing anyone home. That culpability keeps the empty side of Asher's bed warm.

When they finally speak, there's only a hint of venom. "You know I can't stand to have anyone in my space for more than ten minutes."

On the table between them, the candle stutters out, leaving only distant light from the fire. Rowen stares at the smoking wick, her voice little more than a whisper. "That bodes well for us."

Letter #9

I'm starting to think we won't see each other again.

I know it's taken me way too long to admit it, but I guess I wasn't ready to face it. Every Christmas Eve for the past two years, I kept my phone on the pillow and hoped you'd call to send off the season like we used to. You would have laughed if you saw me — or, the old you would have laughed. Since the fight, I don't know if you'd think anything I do is funny.

It was a stupid fight, wasn't it? Looking back, I wish I'd just told my mom about us. About me. I wish I'd done anything but let you leave the cabin. I wish I'd done anything but leave you.

I tried calling Mrs. Norling again to ask about you, but she never called me back. I'm starting to wonder if she's getting my messages, but I'm sure she's just busy with the season.

Oh, and I finally got my own place. I know, it took how many years after I graduated? But my mom got into a wreck just when I saved enough to move out, and she needed help, and it was easier...

I know what you'd say: easier for who?

But you're not here.

Anyway. It's Christmas Eve tonight. I don't think you'll call. I should probably turn my phone off, but I think I'll keep nearby...just in case.

Merry Christmas,
Rowen

Rowen

Things could be worse.

Rowen counts them off as she prepares for bed. For one, she wasn't left outside to face the elements alone. The herd of deer didn't trample her. The bridge didn't collapse with her inside. Asher didn't shoot her as soon as they recognized her, and the two of them have only taken a few pointed jabs at each other.

Certainly, things could be worse...but they could also be better.

Like new texts from her mother. The messages must have come through when Rowen was upstairs, snatching a fraction of signal and stuffing her phone with her mother's disappointment.

What does that mean, Rowen?

I hope you know what an inconvenience this
is. I know you don't care about making things
harder for me, but you've put the Hastings out
as well. You owe them an apology for your
behavior.

Do you know how this makes me look? I try
to do something nice, and you find a way to
ruin it. A good daughter would find a way to
be here, especially on Christmas.

This is why you can't keep a job or a
relationship. I'm sorry, but it's true. You're
selfish. You think of no one but yourself.

Rowen rereads her phone in the dark of the en suite
bathroom and gnaws her bottom lip. She should laugh. She
should find humor in how differently she and her mother view
herself, Rowen the people-pleaser versus the selfish little bitch.
Tears prick the backs of her eyes. Perhaps it would be funnier
if she didn't wonder if the words are true. Her mother says
them often enough; surely there's some validity.

Her mother is sick, for christ's sake. Rowen should be
more upset about that — about *all* of this. Is she so out of touch
that she doesn't realize how horrendous she's being? Her
mother would know, wouldn't she? She's known Rowen her
entire life. After all these years, Rowen thought her mother was
the one with a warped perception, but seeing Asher again fills
Rowen with guilt. Maybe she is cruelly careless with other
people's feelings.

God, and if her mother knew she was spending time with

Asher... Her mother swore up and down that Asher was a bad influence, teaching Rowen to talk back when she went to the mountain every season. It caused a fight with her mother every new year...but it was worth it.

That memory brings a smile to Rowen's face. She turns her phone off. There is no text to ensure she's ok, no concern if she's alive, no increasing panic that she didn't answer.

She knew there wouldn't be.

Perhaps she could slip upstairs and search for that spotty signal to give her mother a call, spill apologies and plead for forgiveness...but what if there was no signal? What if the power outage went farther than the cabin, and a cell tower was knocked out? What if Rowen physically *can't* contact her mother? No one would be the wiser. Nothing Rowen does will make her mother happy, anyway. No matter what, Rowen's missing Christmas, or at least a portion of it. A gallantly-written apology with flowers and groveling would only piss her mother off further. Rowen might as well set her phone aside until she can get off the mountain and deal with the fallout.

There's something freeing about that — about not playing her part. Her heart pounds like when she was a child, sneaking a handful of cereal when her stomach growled long after dinner. Like when she would scurry up to the haven of her room as her mother's key turned in the front door.

So Rowen's break from the real world will be a bit longer than she intended when she took that detour from the main road. That's fine. It was necessary to recharge the best version of herself: the kind and patient Rowen. The Rowen who is energized and pleasant. The Rowen who her mother likes best. Then, once Rowen gets back on the road, her mother will have had time to calm down, and Rowen will be equipped to handle her.

Until then, the only person Rowen has to contend with is Asher.

Easier said than done when there's an invisible *and* physical wall erected between them. Rowen carries her phone and flashlight back into the bedroom, light scattering across the sparsely-decorated space. She should be happy the two of them made it through the first evening. Even with such little distraction, they'd been able to coexist. Both of them were on their best behavior...mostly. No one brought up ancient history, no matter how she — no matter how *either of them* — may have thought about it.

So why does the warmth swarming her stomach feel fresh?

She slips out of her borrowed sweats, tugging on a pair of Asher's spare thermal pajama pants. They're big enough to fit over the swell of Rowen's stomach, clinging to her thick thighs and ass in a way that must be obscene. If Rowen walked out to the living room like this...

Her thighs clench together. God, fresh warmth like *that*, stirring with renewed vigor like it was reborn today instead of left buried where it belonged.

But if Rowen's honest, what happened between the two of them was never buried. It never even died. It was much worse, left bleeding and wounded to suffer and waste away.

Rowen lifts her hair off the back of her neck, suddenly sweltering despite the chill. Her throat tightens as she imagines this thing between them, mauled and emaciated and dwindling into almost-nothingness...but not *complete* nothingness.

Its heart still beat all these years. It still popped into her thoughts when she least wanted it, when a man tucked her hair behind her ear and said she was the perfect woman: pretty and quiet. When a date complimented how easy she was to get along with, because she never voiced her opinions. When a boyfriend admired her loyalty, obedience, and forgiveness, as if she were a dog instead of a woman.

The dying creature cried mournfully until it was all Rowen

could hear: *Asher knew you better than this. Asher didn't want you to cut yourself down just to please them. Asher wanted you wild.*

She clenches her eyes shut, trying to avoid the bleating creature in her mind, but it always crawls out from the shadows. Dragging its body behind it and begging to be put out of its misery — to be put out of Rowen's memory.

Jesus, that's dramatic. She exhales to force the tension from her body, leftover nerves from the sights and sounds outside the cabin. This is reality; there's nothing scary in the forest, and there's nothing between her and Asher. The problems that kept the two of them apart are still there — Asher's heart is still a fortress, and Rowen's voice is still a whisper. Asher is not the long lost love of her life; they are a person who made a quiet life for themself, away from the pain Rowen caused them. Asher doesn't even want to be around someone else. They're happy, or at least content, and she will not disrupt that any more than she already has.

Resolutely, she turns to the bed, which is a challenge of its own. It would be too much to ask for fresh sheets. She's a guest. She will make do with this. She brushes her hand over the familiar quilt, steeling herself to crawl beneath it. In some sick way, she wants to prove this to herself. She wants to put that dying animal into the cold ground once and for all, to show herself she can handle something as simple as Asher's lingering scent.

With a deep breath, she sinks down onto the bed, but the movement fills her nose with their smell: pine and clove and musk.

Too familiar. She jolts back to her feet, watching the darkness under the door. Her movement hasn't caused Asher to stir in the living room. There's nothing but the wind whistling outside. Scowling, Rowen digs her nails into her palm.

Grow up. It's a bed. Get your ass in there.

But her body thrums with possibility. So this is where Asher sleeps — alone, if what they told her at dinner is true. And why wouldn't it be? They have no reason to lie. It's none of her business, but —

For God's sake, Rowen, it's been ten years. Get in the bed!

She clenches her jaw. Mind over matter: the sheets barely smell like them. And that smell barely makes her mouth water, her chest tight, her body ache...

Eventually, she manages to sit and acclimate herself. Then she lies on top of the quilt, then slips her legs beneath, and so on until her head is swimming as she lies rigid under the sheets.

This must be Asher's side; that's why it smells so strongly. When she shifts to the other pillow for a reprieve, she gasps at the overwhelming scent. No: *that* is certainly Asher's side, and Rowen rolls toward the open room to breathe.

It's going to be a long few days...

But she's a glutton for punishment. When her eyes slip shut, her sleepy mind indulges, letting Asher's scent surround her the way it used to. The sheets are warm and soft, tucked up to her chin. She can almost pretend she's back in those old days of the Christmas tree farm, when she had "sleepovers" in Asher's bunk. Her head would tuck under their chin, their fingers tracing lazy patterns under her shirt...

Light blares against her eyelids. Disoriented, Rowen tries to block the blistering glare with her hand. Out the bedroom window, the sun is mostly covered by clouds, but the white snow stretching in all directions brightens everything.

She slept through the night, and then some — and Asher let her.

Probably rather you sleep than wake up and piss them off.

At least their scent waned overnight...or at least, became

more manageable. Groggily, Rowen pulls herself to the bathroom to brush her teeth. On her final rinse, there's a knock at the door.

"Come in!" She wipes at her mouth, wincing at how odd it is to "allow" Asher into their own room.

The door creaks open with them leaning against it. "So Sleeping Beauty *is* awake." Her stomach twists at the teasing, knotting further when Asher's gaze skirts across her face. "Your freckles."

Her cheeks heat. It's been a long time since anyone saw her like this, hair mussed and no makeup before she's had time to prepare for the day. "What about them?"

"Nothing." Asher's fingers curl around the doorknob. "I can just — see them better now. I forgot how many you have."

Rowen's lips part, and Asher's eyes follow them when Bard wriggles his way into the room.

Asher reaches for the scruff of his neck where he squeezes between their legs. "She doesn't want you in here, buddy."

"It's ok." Rowen bends enough to extend her hand, which Bard bounds happily toward. "It's his room more than mine."

"Not while you're here," Asher counters. "Breakfast is on the stove — or lunch, at this point." They raise a saucy brow. "I can heat it up, unless you're planning another twelve-hour nap."

Tauntingly, Rowen tosses her hair back. "I'm considering it...but, seriously, don't worry about me. I can get the food mys-"

Asher doesn't wait for her to finish, shutting the door behind them so she can change. She slips into her borrowed clothes from yesterday, and the scent of eggs and cheese and sausage invites her toward the booth. The spread on the table is quite elaborate for just the two of them. "You made all this without power?"

"It was nothing." Asher sets a plate before her. "I was going to look for the cause of the outage this morning, but I wanted to make sure you didn't need anything before I left."

Her cheeks heat. "Sorry I slept so late."

"Don't be." Is she imagining it, or is there a smirk on Asher's lips? "You must have needed the rest. All that stress from getting stuck up here."

Her fork stops halfway to her mouth. Do they know about last night? About her conflict over sleeping in their sheets? Ducking her head, she forks a bite of egg into her mouth. If anything, she slept because she was *too* relaxed, like the scent of Asher is more potent than lavender.

As she eats, they start cleaning up the dishes.

"Let me do that," she protests. "You've already done so much —"

Without looking up from their work, Asher points toward her. "Guest."

"But —"

"Rowen..." There's that same level tone from last night, the one that sparks heat in Rowen's gut. Asher shakes their head as they scrub. "You're always worried about everyone else. Let me take care of it."

Take care of you.

They don't say the words aloud. Maybe it's Rowen's wishful thinking anyway, so she dabs at her mouth, shooing herself away from the thought. "The food is really good. Again."

Asher half-smiles. "Maybe you're just easily impressed."

Seems Rowen wasn't the only one helped by a good night's sleep. This whole situation is too familiar, sights and sounds and smells slipping her back into old banter. "Two whole recipes in your repertoire? I certainly *am* impressed."

It startles a laugh out of Asher, their mouth falling open in mock offense. "I was going to offer more of my clothes for you to borrow, but now..."

Her stomach somersaults at the implication. They didn't mean anything by it, of course; they won't *actually* keep her naked in their house, just waiting for them to have their way with her...

God, where is her head at? She tries to think of anything but Asher's hands on her bare skin. She really shouldn't use any more of their clothes. The two of them have curves and muscles in very different places. "Did you say there might be some boxes in the attic?" She winces. "I just don't want to stretch your clothes out more than I already have."

Asher's hands still in the sink, suds dripping from their fingers as they curl around the basin. Asher stares into the drain as if they're picturing something before they snap out of it. "We can check..." Asher rinses off the soap. "But any stretching is fine. Doesn't bother me." They dry off their hands, clearing their throat. "Just an excuse for me to bulk up."

That paints a very different visual in Rowen's head, of Asher chopping wood, muscles in their back shifting. Asher carving meat off an animal, biceps flexing under their sleeves. Asher holding themself off of her, hips rolling —

Her fork clatters to the ground. She fumbles for it, but Asher is already beside her with a clean one. "Finish up," they tell her. "Then we'll check the attic."

Rowen

In daylight, the lodge loses a good amount of its creepiness. How had Rowen been so frightened last night? Sunlight streams through every window as they ascend the attic stairs. Asher stands on the top step, sweeping their flashlight over the dust motes swirling through the air. Old portraits lean against the walls, surrounded by furniture draped in sheets next to airtight plastic tubs. Rowen peers over the faded duct tape labels in various handwriting. *Crafts. Books. Games.*

She pops off a plastic lid to find an assortment of worn puzzle boxes. She pulls one out, tracing the familiar illustrations and tape holding the boxes together.

"God, I remember these..." She holds up a box with

nutcrackers aligned in rows. "You remember the season we lost one piece to this, and we couldn't find it until the next year?"

When she looks back over her shoulder, there's something...pained in Asher's expression, but they replace it with haughtiness. "I remember me finishing every puzzle faster than you."

A laugh puffs out of her. "Ever the gracious victor."

Asher places their hands on her hips to shift around her, their breath warm against her ear. "I think *Wild Rowen* might just be a sore loser."

She's not sure what makes her shiver: their body brushing hers, or the mention of her nickname. So they remember it, too, the person Rowen could be when she was here. As Asher moves deeper into the attic, Rowen catches herself smiling. It's so easy to slip back into old habits. Even when things should be tense, even when she can *feel* Asher's resistance, being near them is...relief.

What does it mean that she'd rather be snowed in on a mountain with no electricity than go home to her ailing mother? How can she feel less stressed here than she did in her car, or her apartment, or her office?

She doesn't have an answer. Setting the puzzle back into the box, she brushes dust from her hands. "I wonder if any of my old books are here. I think I started a new one every winter and never finished any of them."

For one reason in particular... Her eyes cling to Asher's receding back as she moves around the center pile, foot catching on a box next to the stair railing. It clatters out of the corner, landing in the pool of light from downstairs. She recognizes the design, even if she can't quite place it. Crouching, she unclasps the lid to reveal a box stuffed with trinkets, dried herbs, and candles.

She beams before she lifts her voice to Asher. "I forgot Mrs. Norling was into this witchy stuff. Do you remember that spell scrapbook she was making?" Rowen's fingers run over a crystal's jagged edge. "I wonder if it's still here..."

She searches deeper inside the tin, fingers closing over a worn leather journal. Its edges are uneven, scraps of paper peeking out at every angle. Grinning, she draws it from the depths and flips through pages of glitter, marker, and construction paper. The spellbook is exactly as she remembers, an amalgam of handwriting and materials, all converged into one.

This scrapbook served as a guest book for the Christmas tree farm. When anyone came to stay, Mrs. Norling invited them to share a bit of magic. There must be notes from all kinds of places in here. Some people wrote a simple line of advice: *throw spilled salt over your left shoulder. Don't trim your nails at night.* But some people filled entire pages with intricate spells.

The ribbon bookmark still clings to the spine, tucked into one of the center pages. Rowen finds the place it's holding, running her fingers over soot stains and wrinkles. This page seems more well-loved than others, like someone spent hours agonizing over it.

Spell of Purpose, it reads. *Just as nature requires both death and life, so do we. Be reborn. When you feel lost and lonely without direction, call on the world around you to return balance. When you feel you have no one, let yourself be filled with divine meaning. When you are ready to shed your old skin, embrace your new identity.*

It certainly sounds like something one of the visitors would write. Rowen scans lower. Beneath the list of ingredients and instructions is a crude image of a hound chasing a stag, just like the picture in the living room. This sketch is pictured from above, two creature's bodies curving as they circle each other.

A frantic note is jotted next to them:

Until magic returns to the mountain. Until our paths converge. Until you let the hound consume your ~~heart hart?~~ heart.

Rowen's mouth twists. What does *that* mean? Did someone see the portrait all those years ago and make up a spell to go with it? It's possible. But the added note at the bottom...Rowen squints. That looks like Asher's handwriting.

The book snaps shut, tugged out of her hands and stuffed back into the metal tin. Asher clamps the lid shut and tucks it under their arm, gaze ducking apologetically. "Sorry..." They run a hand through their hair, turning back to the rest of the attic. "I should give the tin back to Norling. Just — so she has it. You know how she loved this stuff."

Smoke from the page lingers in the air. Rowen brushes her nose, nodding as she rises to her feet. "Of course, yeah." Her mind circles around the spell, but it wouldn't be the first time Asher wrote in the book as a joke. Hell, Rowen had too, searching every year for something mystical to add to the pages. "She'd probably love to see it again."

Asher sets the tin on one of the plastic tubs and hoists them into the air. "Found a few bins of clothes. I'll get your games, too." As they return to the stairs, they shoot her a conciliatory smile. "Maybe you can take the next couple days to improve your puzzle speed."

With a laugh, Rowen follows them downstairs. Once the tubs are in the living room, she pries them open. Most of the clothing is outerwear — snow pants, coats, gloves — but one of the tubs has cozy clothes that look like a perfect fit.

Satisfied, Asher pulls their coat off the hook by the door. "If you're happy with that, I'm going to check the power line."

Rowen rises from the box. "What if I come with you?"

"I told you," Asher shakes their head, "it's not safe for you to go wandering around out there." There's something off in the depths of their eyes, but they keep it locked away. "Besides, it's boring shit. You don't want to trudge around in the snow for hours."

"I'll make dinner, then." The words escape her before she really considers them. "As thanks for letting me stay."

Asher turns in the doorway, bracing their hand against it as they scrutinize her. "What is it gonna take to get you to act like a guest?"

"Not a guest by choice," she mutters. Asher's brow furrows, and she realizes her mistake. "I meant not by *your* choice —"

"In any case…" Asher steps closer, fixing Rowen under a firm gaze. "You can do whatever you want in here for fun, but do not lift a finger for me. No cooking. No cleaning. Nothing to be a 'good guest.'"

Her mouth clamps shut. It's like they read her mind and heard the nagging thoughts in her mother's voice. *You owe them. Act like you have some manners! God, have I taught you nothing…*

Her heart trips over itself. "I'll make mulled wine, then." Their head tilts humorlessly. It's a way to skirt their rules, and they know it. "You used to like it," Rowen insists. "Besides, I saw the ingredients in the pantry. One puzzle isn't going to last me for the eight hours you're gone."

Asher's eyes roll. "It won't be that long this time." They look down their nose at her, searching for a tell. "Is this an excuse to sneak in some holiday cheer? Because you're depressed I was going to be here alone on Christmas?"

It's difficult to think with their attention focused on her. She tries to keep her eyelashes from fluttering, heat pooling in her face. "At least you can be drunk during the festivities. Drown out all the Christmas spirit."

Asher watches her mouth form around the words,

lingering even after she finishes. "Fine. Make your mulled wine." They reach behind them to back out the door. "But that's the extent of it. No searching the woods for greenery. No baking cookies. No Christmas carols. I don't want Bard picking up any bad habits."

She doesn't miss the amusement in their eyes as they cross the threshold. Her teeth dig into her lips when she smiles. "There's no telling what we'll get up to if you're gone all day."

Asher leans back inside, setting their face in front of hers. "I'll be back before the sun sets. Time me."

She's struck with the sudden urge to press her mouth against theirs. It's a giddy, silly thought, as if they're leaving for work and she's kissing them goodbye. Abruptly, she stops herself, pressing her lips into a thin line as she waves after them.

The power's back on within a few hours. Between her puzzle and the wine, Rowen rifles through the tubs of clothing and finds an old nightgown she remembers. It barely covers her ass now, but it serves as a breathable shirt between her sweater and leggings. And Asher keeps their word, pushing through the front door as light begins to fade. Rowen stirs the ladle through the wine, struck with the same odd feeling she had in the doorway, as if she's living another life.

After dinner, Bard retires to the main bedroom for his pre-sleep nap. Even with the power back on, neither of them turn on the lights. Candles are better Christmas atmosphere anyway. Rowen brings two mugs into the living room, and Asher steps back from the crackling fireplace to take their first sip.

"Damn. Alright." Throat bobbing, they swallow again, hissing from the heat. "The wine was a good call."

Smugly, Rowen curls her feet beneath her on the couch. "Maybe you should let your *guest* do more for you."

Asher settles back on the other side of the couch, holding

their mug by the rim. "Tastes just like I remember."

Rowen holds her mug between her hands, head tilting wistfully. "Just like bonfire nights."

Asher's gaze clings to the flames, voice low between them. "We never lasted very long at the bonfire."

The memory warms Rowen's throat and chest, spilling over her ribs until she feels like she's glowing from the inside. No, they never did stay long at the bonfires. The two of them always stumbled away together, Asher's cold fingers making Rowen squeal before they made her groan...

Asher seems to shake off the memory, peering into their mug before they set it on the coffee table. "I checked the lake today." Their voice has lost that sultry dip, returning to something more reserved. "Not frozen yet, but it should be thick enough in a day or so. You'll be able to get across it."

Disappointment weaves through Rowen's chest. It's so much easier when she doesn't remember this is temporary. Technically, it's a setback...for both of them. In a few days, she'll have to face what she's been putting off. What she has to go back to. What she's leaving behind.

She sets her half-finished mug on the table. "We should play a game." Her voice is tight when she rises to her feet, so she tries to flatten it into something normal. "Since we're already in the festive spirit, despite your best efforts."

Asher narrows their eyes, but they don't deny her. "What do you have in mind?"

She tries to keep her thoughts in line. *It's just a game. Just for fun. Just for something to do.* "Bet I can still beat you at Christmas Slap."

A challenge flickers in Asher's eyes. "Get the cards."

Eleven

Asher

Asher is fine. Asher is under control. Asher is not in danger of slipping.

They had a good excuse to get out of the lodge today, but the Voice in their head was oddly silent. They're not sure what that means. Is the Voice tired from yesterday, or is it saving its strength to burst out at the worst possible moment?

Asher was waiting for it when Rowen found the spellbook in the attic. That one book is almost as damning as what Asher has hidden under the floorboards upstairs. When they saw Rowen was flipped to the very page that ruined their life, Asher nearly choked. All they can do is pray she's as confused by the muddled "prophecy" as they are. It's how they reassure themself now that the tin is hidden again. Rowen doesn't know what any of the spellbook markings mean. She doesn't know what Asher is. She doesn't know that Norling gave Asher the book before she left, hoping the very thing that got Asher into this mess might get them out of it.

But like everything else, the spellbook is another dead end.

Asher doesn't want to think about it. Thinking about it only gives it power, much like Asher's dangerous thoughts about Rowen. They tamp down on those thoughts as she carries a pack of cards back to the coffee table. It's good they found those boxes in the attic, because seeing her in *their* clothes was stirring up things they would rather not deal with.

Not that watching Rowen cozied up in a sweater is doing anything to put their mind at ease.

She kneels on the carpet, lifting her brows toward them on the couch. "You remember how to play?"

They swallow roughly. *Do not think about her on her knees. Do not think about —* "You should've picked a harder game if you really wanted to beat me."

"Let's make it more interesting, then, since we're in the festive spirit." A coy smile flickers on her lips. "Winner is crowned the King of Misrule..." She pauses uncertainly. "If you'd accept the title."

It's been ages since Asher heard that name, not that they ever earned the crown. Back in the day, the farm staff relegated a new King every week, someone to lead them in drinking games and harmless mischief. One girl was elected more than anyone else. "Reminiscing on your glory days?" Asher scoffs.

"I tried to rig it for you!" Rowen reminds them as she deals the cards. "But you always sabotaged it, even when you were sulking over not being picked."

Sabotaged. Asher tries not to let the word strike them, taking a drink to hide their face. "I didn't need the pity. No one trusted me to be in charge of some Christmas tradition, anyway."

"I did."

Heat spreads through Asher's body. They take another long sip, avoiding Rowen's gaze as she continues dealing. They've barely had a quarter of their drink, but their head already feels light and bubbly. Rowen's presence here upsets the balance Asher struck with this place — functioning but unrecognizable, physically present but mentally distant to keep the memories at bay. With Rowen here again, warmth creeps in where Asher didn't expect it: flickering candles, seasonal wine, a glow from the fire and the drinks and her smile.

She clacks her cards into an organized pile. "Ready?"

Maybe Asher has forgotten the rules of the game, but Rowen is kind enough to remind them. That's her downfall, though: too nice as always. Asher picks the game back up like those nights on the farm were just yesterday, slowly adding to the winning stack on their side of the table.

When Rowen loses her final card, her spine straightens. "The first game was a trial run."

Victoriously, Asher shuffles the cards. "Whatever you say."

The next game turns into two out of three, then three out of five, until the score is so close that they both lose track. Maybe the refilled drinks are to blame for that, as well as the laughing arguments and rule dissections and poor attempts at cheating.

It all comes down to the final game. It's been a tight race, but a winner has to be declared. Rowen chews her lip as her cards fade slowly until she's left with only one. Eyes shut, she grips the card in her hand before she flips it over onto the pile.

It's a double.

Her eyes widen, hand darting toward it — but Asher is faster, grinning at the sting of her palm smacking the back of their hand. She makes an affronted noise as they swipe the last of her cards and lean back mockingly. "Someone's lost her touch! What would people say if they knew you'd lost your streak to little ol' me?"

"Always a humble winner." Sneering prettily, Rowen lifts her half-empty glass. "I concede, your Majesty."

Asher's eyes narrow skeptically. "You let me win."

"I did not! The mulled wine is just...a little stronger than I remember." She polishes off the rest of her glass, stained tongue dragging over her lips as she folds her hands on the coffee table. "So what is your first royal decree?"

Asher's toes curl in their socks. Firelight dances behind Rowen's hair, making her eyes look even darker, keeping Asher pinned under her gaze. What had been cozy moments before now feels sweltering, sweat pricking along Asher's back. "I don't know..." They lean back against the couch, heat spreading low in their gut. "This whole thing is..." They bite their tongue to quell the urge to ruin this. It would be easy to say this is silly, to retreat outside under the guise of work, to put space between them and Rowen's glowing face.

You always sabotaged it.

The flames pop. Rowen lifts the hair off the back of her neck, avoiding their gaze as if the fire's in their eyes and not behind her. "God, it's hot in here," she breathes.

"Only if you're drunk, lightweight."

"I am *not* drunk."

They don't know why she says it like that. Why she needs them to know she's not intoxicated, her eyes locking onto theirs and refusing to budge. It feels...challenging. Asher brings their mug to their mouth. "Take off your sweater, then."

Fuck. They don't know why they said it. Rowen's lips part, cheeks darkening. Silence fills the room until there's hardly space to breathe, until Asher's chest is tight and their body's hot.

"To cool off," Asher adds, tonguing the rim of their mug. "So you don't overheat."

Her look is glassy, headier than the wine. "If the King wills it."

The words nearly force a groan out of Asher. Rowen tugs the thick fabric over her head, hair clinging with static when she discards the garment. Asher's fingers curl. So that's what she's wearing underneath it. A nightgown from one of the bins, gauzy and thin and the slightest bit transparent.

"Better?" Asher croaks.

"Still hot," she pants. Her chest rises and falls, nipples peaking against the fabric.

Asher struggles to keep their voice even. "Pants off, too, then."

She does exactly as they say, rising onto her knees to slip the leggings off. Now there's nothing between them but the gauzy fabric that barely covers her ass. Her voice is soft and sultry. "What else would you have me do?"

It's too tempting. Too fucking tempting to command her to strip off the last bit of clothing, to see her freckled shoulders covered in firelight and a flush and nothing else. But Asher's jaw clenches as they tear their eyes away.

"You're the King," Rowen reminds them, like she's trying to hold onto this moment, like she wants them to direct her just as badly as they do. "Do your worst."

It's too much, too hot, too close, like the massive cabin is closing in to push them together. Of course it would, when Asher can't have her. When they aren't fit to be near her. When they've been dying to play this game, but they can never win.

Their lip curls derisively. "You couldn't handle my worst."

The tension of their locked eyes feels like it could tear the entire cabin in half...but there's nothing. No earth-shattering event. No chasm opening beneath their feet, just Rowen backlit by the fire, and Asher's heart in their throat.

Carefully, she pushes to her feet, dress brushing the tops of those gorgeous thighs. "Maybe I could give you some ideas.

Since I have experience."

Amusement flutters in Asher's chest before it's drowned by molten desire. God, that gown is so fucking *short*, teasing them with the thought of what lies beneath it.

Rowen reaches the furthest arm of the couch, trailing her nails along it. "You could make me walk out in the snow. Freeze my ass off for a minute."

Asher tilts their head back to keep her in sight. "Maybe I should. You look a little *flushed*."

She circles behind them, and the hair on their neck stands like they're an animal in the forest. She lowers her head next to theirs, blocking their peripheral.

"You could have me feed you something." Her smile spreads in the corner of their eyes. "Cornmeal. Raw meat. The least festive thing you can think of."

Asher's teeth dig into their grin as she finally circles beside them, her gaze trailing down their body. Her mouth opens before it shuts again, lips pressed tightly together.

"Tell me." They need to hear it. They need to know if her mind's in the same place, their fingers twitching toward her bare skin.

Her throat bobs before she whispers. "A King should have something pretty in their lap."

It takes all Asher has not to shift in their seat, not to show the effect the thought has on them. They force their arms to spread along the back of the couch, refusing the ache between their legs. Fuck, they're really taking 'enjoying themselves for a few days' to a new level. "This seems familiar."

Rowen sucks in a breath. So she remembers it, too — the first time they ever crossed that line. Beautiful Rowen in a crown of holly, stumbling over to Asher in a corner of a party. This isn't that night, but it stirs with the same promise. A crackling fire and fierce competition, stoking heat that reminds them both of when they were closer.

Rowen's fingers trace the line of their jaw, so light it could almost be their imagination. "Do you want me?"

It's exactly what she said the first time, Wild Rowen emboldened on wine and desire. She could have had anyone at that party, but her gaze stuck on Asher, as if she knew the flaring emotion they were trying to resist. They had watched her for weeks, clenching their fists every time one of the boys flirted with her. Asher tried to bury their hunger and keep their distance, even as the gaping pit inside them begged to be filled. Begged for *her*.

The night of the party, Rowen stopped just watching. She slotted their fingers together, staring at Asher's surly barriers as if she knew she could scale them. *You have to show me.* Her voice was so soft, just for them. *If you want me to stay, you have to show me —*

Their body had reacted before they could think, fingers tightening around hers as their legs dipped open in invitation.

Just like now. History repeats itself, their hand curling over hers to guide her around the arm of the couch. She hitches her skirt, sinking down to straddle one of Asher's thighs.

Her face hovers before them, hair glowing like a fiery halo. Their head swims from the wine and her body pressed against them. This can't be real. They can't let themself believe it, because it's been hopeless for so long. It takes all they have to keep from touching her, their arms draped over the back of the couch. If they reach out, she'll disappear; they know that from every dream they've had for the past ten years.

But tonight, she is real. She is here, delving into the past and reliving the moment Asher has replayed in their mind again and again.

Her hands tremble as she searches for somewhere to place them, as if she has the same fear. The moment is getting to her too, pulling both of them through time until it's hard to say what's "now" and what was "then." It feels like magic. Are they reenacting the past? Are they caught up in ancient history? Are these old feelings shaking off the dust, or has something been reignited?

The vibrant current through Asher's limbs tells them their answer.

One of Rowen's hands settles on the arm of the couch, her other gripping the back to keep herself off Asher's chest. If they both keep their hands to themselves, it's safer...as if she isn't warm in their lap. As if they can hear anything but the racing of their pulse.

All those years ago, they watched her desperately from afar...but she was watching them, too. She saw them try to keep from melting for her, but it was no use then.

It's no use now.

Rowen shifts her hips in the slightest circle. "You can be mean, if it makes it easier." Her whisper is just like it was before, precarious and reckless and wild. "I think I like it."

Twelve

Asher

Asher hisses between their teeth. When Rowen rolls against their thigh, that weak pit inside them pleads for more. Their tongue itches to drag against her throat, to lap into her mouth, to swallow everything she offers.

But they can't do that. They shove down that needy feeling to reach for the hardened edges they can handle. Coolly, their gaze drags down to the melting point where their bodies meet. A laugh stirs low in their throat. "Are you this desperate to fuck my leg?"

Rowen shudders. They *are* mean, voice searing with degradation they haven't touched in so long. She wasn't lying when she said she liked it, hips stuttering as she tries to hide her whimper.

Beneath the dress, Asher grips her waist. "*Do not stop.*" Something possessive claws into their voice, eyes blazing when they lock with hers. "*That's* my royal fucking decree. You remember the safeword?"

Her breath trembles. "Tinsel."

They almost laugh. They should never have let her pick that festive fucking word, but from the spread of her pupils, she's nowhere near saying it. Nails digging into her flesh, Asher goads her on. "Until you say that, keep riding my fucking thigh until I tell you to stop."

A moan tears out of her. Obediently, she circles against their sweats, a sinful motion that drags Asher's mind to the past. The two of them weren't just like this the first night; it was every night. In the front seat of the pickup while everyone else slept in their beds. Behind the blanket draped around Asher's bunk to "keep out the cold." Lying in the snow while Asher jerked her pants to her knees and pulled her cunt against their tongue.

But tonight on this couch is brand new. It's not a recreation; Asher wants her *now*. They guide her in a rhythm that builds like the whine in her throat as her fingers dig into the couch.

"Have you been thinking about this?" Cruelty curls in Asher's tone. "Dry humping in the living room? You don't even need me here. You could do this with anything: the arm of the couch. Your pillow. *My* pillow." A filthy thought springs like a trap in their mind. "Have you already done it, Rowen? Have you been fucking the pillows in my bed and pretending they're me?"

God, the humiliation works just like it used to, snatching a whimper from her mouth. Her hips work faster, as if she can outrun it. Outrun *them*. Little does she know, Asher is hot on the trail of her arousal.

They pull their hands from her hips so she has to do all the work herself. "You're making a mess on my pants. Look..." With one hand, they force her eyes down to where she grinds a wet spot against the fabric. "Are you even wearing panties? You're fucking *soaked*, princess."

Fuck, they've missed calling her that. She bites back a sob, grinding figure-eights against the juncture of their hip. It's like she needs more than their thigh, more than their chests pressed together, more than her head cradled against their chest.

"Why is that, Rowen?" They grip her hair tight at the root, keeping their mouth close to her ear. "Didn't get what you need out in the real world? Finance bros and former frat boys don't do it for you?"

Her mouth buries against their shoulder.

They tug her back. "Do not make a sound where I can't hear it. I want every pathetic little noise echoing off these walls."

Her hips pick up speed like they're keeping pace with the thoughts in Asher's head: *I want your groans painted across this cabin. I want your cries buried in the wall. I never want to get you out.*

"Bet those boyfriends fuck you every way they know how." Asher's lips pout mockingly. "But it's not enough, is it? They're too vanilla, even for sweet little Rowen." Asher's fingers tighten in her hair. "They're too bland, because you're too busy thinking about this. Because riding my leg is better than anything they do to you."

Her fingers curl in the front of their shirt. It stretches out of shape, but they don't care as long as Rowen leaves her mark.

Something predatory slinks through their chest, coiling into their voice. "What do they try with you, huh? What do you like these days?" With the hand in her hair, they press their arm against her spine, keeping her close to their body so all she can move is her hips. "Bet they want you to call them 'Daddy,' don't they? And you do it, even though they haven't earned it. Even though they can barely make you moan."

Her hips stutter when she sobs, "How do you *know*?"

Blood pulses through Asher's ears. "Don't insult me." Their voice almost sounds wounded, dipping low as they enunciate every word. "I know you. I knew you ten years ago. I haven't stopped." Every circle of her hips, every breath from her chest, every word against their skin makes them *burn*. "And I'm not your 'Daddy.' I'm your fucking *King*. I'm the God of this entire fucking mountain."

Only now does Asher realize the Voice is thrumming through their head, slipping out of their mouth until it sounds like them. It's tangled with their carnal thoughts, the ink on their throat smoldering as words spill. For a panicked moment, Asher fears the change is coming — but the Voice doesn't press out against their skin. It clings to Rowen's desire, as if it's as enraptured by her as Asher is.

She whimpers against them, clutching at their shirt as she works her hips. They should stop this. They should pull away to keep the danger of the Voice at bay...but they want her just as much as it does. *More.* Forehead pressed to hers, they drag their nose against her neck.

She smells like *ours*.

A low growl builds in their chest, but they're not sure whose it is — theirs or the Voice. "'*Do your worst.*'" Hot and hateful, they taunt her earlier request, teeth scraping her throat. "You couldn't handle ugly, princess. You can't even begin to picture it, because everything about you is perfect. Perfect image. Perfect demeanor." When their fingers dig into the thick flesh of her thighs, their groan vibrates against her. "Perfect fucking *body*."

Her nails drag down their chest. They can't help themself, laving their tongue against her pulse as if they can taste it, as if every beat buzzes through them and fills them with *her*.

"Keep riding me," they rasp. "Don't you fucking stop."

Her legs shake as if Asher is the only thing keeping her upright, the only thing solid enough to cling to.

They hold her hair back, keeping her throat exposed to them. "So pretty when you're about to come." The Voice rises like a tidal wave, screaming through their head. **Let me have her. Let me devour her.** *"Let me have it!"*

They force the Voice back down, drowning in the sounds of Rowen's release. It's so much better than they remember. When she comes this time, her mouth is filled with curses and whimpers, fingers clutching for them as if she could claw her way under their skin. As if she could burrow in deep and stay in their chest the way she has for the last ten years.

Her breath begins to even against their cheekbone. Distantly, they realize the hand gripped in her hair has started brushing through her curls. Her eyelashes flutter against their clavicle, exposed by the stretched collar of their henley.

They've gotten too comfortable. The Voice is still near, weaving dangerously through Asher's head until Asher's not sure who the thoughts belong to. Asher can't be this close to Rowen. Not when something monstrous lives inside them. What would happen if it clawed its way out? What if the Voice took a chance to consume her? What if it shredded through the few inches of skin between them?

Asher shifts their weight beneath her, laughter hoarse in their throat. "I should make you clean up the mess you made." It's an easy out, a way for both of them to pry themselves apart and remember what they're doing here. They're trapped together for a few days. This was a horny slip-up. They don't owe each other more than that. *She* doesn't owe them more than that.

But Rowen doesn't blush and pull away. Instead, she sinks to her knees on the floor and meets their eyes. She isn't settling back into tentative propriety. She isn't taking the easy way out.

Her pink tongue lays flat before it drags over the wet spot she left.

Asher's stomach seizes, an animal groan budding in their throat. Her tongue travels higher, up their thigh to the juncture between their legs. She waits for them to say the word, her gaze locked on theirs before her hot mouth closes over them.

Their knees go weak. She's never touched them like this. They never let her, always focused on *her*, but the body they have now isn't shy of these touches. Wet heat spreads through their core at the pleading look in Rowen's eyes, the way she waits for them, the way she —

They grip her hair to pull her back, chest heaving as the Voice screams obscenities in their head.

"I need to — bring in more firewood." Avoiding her eyes, Asher pushes to their feet, guiding her head out of the way with a gentle hand. "You should get some sleep."

They can't look at her any longer, because god, what would they do? Break the promises they made to themself. Put her in danger with this thing inside them. Moving to the door, Asher jerks on an outer coat, shoving their feet into boots and stepping out into the cold.

Wind tears through the thin fabric of their pants. Head down, they barrel toward the shed, gritting their teeth as the Voice forces its way to the front of their skull. It doesn't speak words that Asher understands. It screams and brays like a dying animal, gut-wrenching sounds Asher can't even hope to translate. They understand the meaning, though: frustration. Desperation. Mourning.

The Voice refuses to stay quiet. It screeches through Asher just as they feared, making the metal siding warp when they stagger against the shed. The Voice won't stay inside. It's rising to the surface, and Asher has to get away. They have to keep this beast far from Rowen.

They shed their clothes at the door as pain shreds through

their body. Carnal anger punches up through their skin, dragging Asher through the snow as they wrestle with the furious creature.

Past the animal shrieking, only one coherent thought pulses through them.

The more you fight, the worse it gets.

Thirteen

Asher

The Voice makes Asher remember. Every bone in their body breaks, skin tearing as they lurch through the trees. Snow hurtles around them, but the Voice holds Asher's face against the memory until it burns. Ten years was not long enough to dull the ache. There is no pain like reliving.

There is no contentment like the night before Christmas Eve.

Not that Asher would admit it. On the tree farm, the last remaining families have checked out and driven back down the mountain. This afternoon, the staff cleaned the lodge from top to bottom, storing equipment until next November. Norling bid them all goodnight with a knowing glint in her eye. "Stay *safe*. And don't stay up too late. I'm making breakfast before you leave tomorrow."

The group agreed, but they won't get any sleep tonight. It's the last night of the season, when the staff throw together a bonfire and reminisce. It's also the last night Asher gets to fall asleep next to Rowen, her warm body curled against them beneath the quilt.

On the snowy trail, a group of staff members pass Asher. "Hacksaw champion!" Daniel shouts. The others raise their thermoses in appreciation as Daniel claps Asher on the shoulder. "Thought we were fucked when the chainsaw ran out of gas. Never seen a tree come down that fast."

Asher laughs, joy springing in their chest. "You flatterer."

"I owe you a beer at the bonfire!" Daniel calls. "Better get there before I drink them all. I'll save one for your *friend*, too."

The group crows delightedly. Asher waves them off with a smile that captures their entire face.

The farm feels like home this season. Asher bonds with new staffers, reconnects with the old, and spends hours in the forest's tranquility. Every day feels bright and shiny, an oasis from the rest of the world.

It wouldn't have been like this if not for Rowen. Just the thought of her makes Asher hunch their shoulders against the wind, grinning into their collar. When she approached them at that party a few years ago, they should have known it would become something bigger. What started as tentative hope has opened Asher to happiness they weren't sure they could reach.

When they make it to Rowen's cabin, they knock in a familiar rhythm. The answer from inside is quiet. Asher pushes open the door to find Rowen seated on her bottom bunk.

"You ready? I got your favorite." Asher tips a flask into view, wiggling their fingers spookily. "Liquid courage in case Natasha tells one of her scary stories again."

When Rowen smiles, Asher stiffens. That's not her real

smile. That's the smile she uses when she deals with rude customers. When she takes on extra chores. When she gets off the phone with her mother.

Asher's hand drops. "What's wrong?"

Rowen re-folds the blanket at the end of her bed. "My mom wants me home before lunch tomorrow."

Asher's face falls. That means the two of them won't have their usual tradition. It's not much, but stopping at the shops along the mountain before one last lunch was what Asher looked forward to all season. It's probably the last year they'll get to do it, too...but Rowen's already glum enough. "That's ok." Asher leans against her bunk. "Few more months, and you'll graduate. Then she can't hold tuition over your head."

Rowen avoids Asher's gaze. "She wants me to come home early...because she wants me to meet a boy."

Asher's stomach twists anxiously. "Meet a boy, like...to date?"

Rowen nods. It's far from the first time her mother has stuck a hand in Rowen's life to rearrange it.

Asher's jaw tightens. "What did you say?"

"I don't know..." Rowen wipes at her eyes. "It's just one date, right? I'll meet him and be nice until my mom loses interest." Finally, Rowen lifts her face and reaches for Asher's hand. "It won't mean anything. It's just easier to keep my mom happy."

Jealousy heats Asher's neck. They inch back from her. "Easier for who?"

Rowen's expression looks bruised. "Easier for *us*. If she found out I'm..." Her lip trembles. She can't even say it. Then again, Asher can't pinpoint what *they* are either, but at least they know it's something different. "If she found out, she'd make sure we couldn't see each other. She'd cut off my phone. She'd take my car. She'd kick me out. She has all my documents: social security, birth certificate... She'd stop paying my tuition, and I'm so close to graduating..." Fingers trembling, Rowen's hand flits to her mouth as she draws a steadying breath. "I don't have enough saved to take all of that on at once."

"We could figure it out." Asher kneels beside her, squeezing her knee. "Hell, I got kicked out of my parents' house, and I figured it out...eventually." Never mind the screaming fights and scraping by and things they had to leave behind. "You wouldn't have to do it by yourself, Rowen."

Her brows knit, turning her eyes up to theirs. "Wouldn't I?" When Asher only blinks, Rowen shakes her head, staring at the cabin floorboards. "How could I tell my mom anything? You won't even tell me how you feel."

Asher's throat tightens. "What are you talking about?" Their heart thuds guiltily. They know exactly what she means, but they've been putting it off, trying not to dig into the parts of themself they don't want to look at.

Look at them, the Voice commands.

Hooves beat the ground somewhere beneath Asher. They are fleeing. Always fleeing.

Look at us.

Look at me.

"What are we?" Rowen gestures weakly. They've had this conversation before. "What are we doing?"

"We care about each other." Asher's voice sounds far away, repeating the words to assuage themself. "We're spending time together."

"But we only see each other once a year. We only see each other *here*," Rowen pleads. "You won't visit me on campus —"

"I told you, it's not my scene —"

"You won't let me visit *you*."

"I'm saving up for a better place!" Asher swallows roughly.

"A few more months, and it'll be ready, I promise." That's what they said three months ago, before their apartment flooded. That's what they said four months before that. They just want their space to be good enough. To be perfect. That's what Rowen deserves. That's what she's used to.

If Asher fears disappointing her the way they disappoint everyone, that's secondary.

But Rowen sees them as she always does. Her hands cup their jaw, tilting them gently toward her. "Why won't you let me in?" Her eyes flit between both of theirs, as if she might find the answer unguarded in their gaze. "I told you how I feel about you. I told you that I *love* you."

The word makes Asher flinch. They've heard it too many times from other people. *I love you, that's why I'm doing this. That's why I can't stand by and watch the choices you've made. That's why you're not welcome here anymore...*

Their heart pulses like a train careening off the tracks. Asher learned a long time ago that no one will stand by them. Not when it matters. Not when things are hard or ugly or scary. They can't need this. They can't need *her*. They're too close already.

Raw words spill out of their mouth. "Whatever. It doesn't matter. We don't need to keep pretending this is..."

Rowen's wounded breath makes Asher want to fall at her feet.

They fight to keep their expression still, but their eyes sting. "I mean, what are we doing? It's the last winter you're gonna be here anyway. In a few months, you'll get a brand new job. You'll probably move away. You *should* move away, so you can get away from your mom." They feel robotic, like they've removed themself from their body, like this is the only way to speak without crying. "Otherwise, you'll be stuck living under her forever. You have to stand up to her sometime. We were kidding ourselves to think we could keep doing this."

Rowen watches her hands as if something has slipped through her fingers. For a moment, Asher thinks she won't say anything. That she'll bow her head and go along with someone else's bridle, *again*. That she won't fight it. That she won't fight for *them*.

Ears ringing, Asher rises to their feet.

"You're pushing me away." Rowen's voice is shaky, but she lifts it to make sure Asher hears. "You act like you don't care, but I know you do. I *know* it." Her lip trembles, fingers curling into her sweater, like she desperately wants the words to be true. "But I don't know why you're doing this. Are you trying to sabotage it? Is that it?" Her lip trembles as she meets their gaze. "You're trying to hurt yourself, but you're hurting *me*."

Shame courses through them. They *are* hurting her, a wounded creature lashing out at a gentle hand. Is this what it's like to be known? To be seen? To feel all of their skin pulled back, exposing the weakness underneath?

They can't show that to Rowen. They can't force her to wade through every prickly, thorny part of them. The parts they don't understand. The parts that crave her too deeply. The parts that need her so badly, they would devour her whole.

You always had that hunger for affection, the Voice rumbles. **Even before me.**

Air thins in Asher's lungs. They gallop through the woods, away from the Voice and the memory.

I did as you asked. The Voice always follows. **I severed that appetite from you. I took on that wanting, so you would not have to bear it. I grew into that yearning, gaping pit.**

Cries spill from Asher's snout, inhuman sounds that tear through the wind. The Voice only grows louder.

I became that voracious part of you, and still, you starve me.

The pit screams and cries inside them.

Rowen's voice is soft and shattered. "Don't run from me."

But Asher is already off into the snow.

Fourteen

Rowen

Rowen isn't surprised that Asher left her alone.

She hasn't moved from her spot in front of the couch, trying not to remember what the two of them just did. Getting snowed in here may have been more risky than taking her chances out in the wild.

Maybe she should be more upset that Asher took off, but she only has herself to blame. She knows this side of Asher, the panicked look on their face when she sank to the ground. They've never let her close to their body. It's always been *them* touching *her*, them stirring heat with their mouth or fingers, them whispering filthy, beautiful things about her body.

They don't let her do the same. Never stripping out of their clothes, never letting her touch their bare skin, never allowing her to bring them pleasure the way they give it to her.

Sinking to her knees was a risky move. Without the weight of their chests pressed together, the two of them had to look at each other. They both had to face the reality that they'd gotten sucked into each other while the night had spiraled out of control.

And Asher has never been good at letting anyone close. There was a time when it seemed like they were opening up, but it's clear that part of them was shed in the last ten years.

Fooling around with Asher on the couch was just that: fooling around. It was lust fanning desire, an old flame flaring up again. Neither of them have gotten over their physical chemistry, nor the excuses they made for why it couldn't continue all those years ago.

They're stuck in the past in more ways than one.

But knowing that doesn't make Rowen feel any less alone or abandoned. The fireplace crackles behind her, the sound of the front door slamming still echoing in her head. Her chest twinges with an old hurt, a straining muscle she hasn't used in so long. It's silly for her to feel wounded. It's been ten years; she knew that when she toed the line and offered herself into Asher's lap. One steamy night doesn't change anything.

Her mind circles around the same questions: *Are we the same people we were? Is it worse if we are, or if we're not?*

Once she gets her shaky legs beneath her, she makes her way into the bedroom and goes through the motions: shower, brushing teeth, climbing into bed. Sleep evades her for hours, touch-and-go through the night as Bard's warm body curls against her. In the morning, he's escaped to the living room, but Asher is nowhere to be seen. They must have come back sometime in the morning, leaving a note in the kitchen to point her toward leftovers. They'll be working late into the night, of course.

Doing what, she can't even imagine. She's beginning to

think they just stand in the barn for hours, finding any excuse to stay away from her. She could go looking for them. It's a tempting thought, but even the note they left underlined a singular command: *Stay inside.*

Her night of restless sleep proves useful. She passes the hours dozing on the couch between movies and a workbook of word and number games. At dusk, she eats dinner alone, feeding Bard little scraps and watching out the window for signs of Asher. Save for birds flying off from the trees, there's no movement.

For all she knows, Asher might be watching the lodge and waiting for her to sleep so they can sneak in unnoticed. A rebellious part of her wants to sit up waiting for them, to confront them about avoiding her, but what would she say? She's a guest. They're giving her space and making sure she has what she needs. What happened last night certainly isn't part of their hosting duties, and no doubt they're counting down the days until she's out of their hair. So Rowen turns in for the evening, leaving Bard napping on the couch.

Sleep comes much easier tonight, wrapping her in its arms and dragging her down into its depths. It's warm and comfortable, filling her nose with pine and cloves. Her stomach twinges. It's the scent of Asher's sheets, but stronger, like she's pressing her face against their neck. Something warm and wet drags over her skin, making her whimper. It's both animal and not, a creature with warm breath huffing from its nostrils. In the dark of her mind, the creature paws the ground, mouthing against her throat as if the rush of her blood is enough to make it lose control.

Just like Asher did last night. An ache starts between her legs, forcing her thighs together as a moan slips past her lips. That sound rouses her from sleep, blinking in the dark as she tries to get her bearings. There is no creature, just Asher's sheets tangled around her legs and a desperate desire in the pit of her stomach.

She checks her phone; it's after three. Surely Asher has returned by now, sleeping only feet away from her in the living room. If she gets up early enough, she can catch them...but not this early. Besides, there's an even more pressing need seeping through her body. She tries to fight off temptation, biting her lip and willing the dreamy desire away, but her fingers travel down over her round stomach.

Even when she shuts her eyes, she can't pretend it's Asher's hands on her. Her fingers are too short, nails too sharp, skin too smooth. She wishes she could remember exactly where the calluses on Asher's hands are. They've gained new ones in the years since they last touched her. On the couch, she barely got a taste when they brushed her arms and guided her hips. God, she wants to memorize every rough place on their body and drag her mouth over them...

Her teeth grit. Maybe she shouldn't do this. Maybe she shouldn't get herself off in their bed, no matter what they hinted at on the couch...but it's not like they'll keep the same sheets on their bed after she leaves.

Or will they? Her eyes clench shut at the prospect. No: Asher will wash their sheets to get rid of every remnant of her...or maybe they want to smell the two of them together, their scents mingling, hers needy and wanton and wasted on wanting them.

When she dips her fingers between her legs, the slick sound makes her gasp. God, she should be embarrassed. Asher hasn't been near her for an entire day, but the thought of them alone is enough to get her like this. Maybe they'll hear her whimpers from the living room. Maybe they'll pull themself up from the couch, press their ear to the door and turn the knob —

Something slams against the cabin. Rowen yelps, springing to her feet as a portrait clatters to the ground. Her heart thuds as she holds her breath, trying to hear past her pulse to whatever is outside...

There is no other sound. Rowen stays frozen, watching the darkness outside the window, begging her eyes to see something in the infinite snow and shadows.

If she reaches the flashlight on the nightstand... Her hand clenches at her side. What if seeing what's out there is worse? She swallows. There's still no motion outside the window. Surely the sound woke Asher. Carefully, Rowen toes along the floorboards, pushing the fallen portrait aside as she tugs the door open.

The living room is dark, the fire burned out long ago. An eerie feeling twists and turns up her spine. Where is Asher?

At the front door, something scratches and whines. When she squints, she can make out Bard's paws against the wood. He grows louder when a massive shadow passes by the window.

Rowen bites her tongue to keep from screaming. Insistently, Bard barks and jumps at the movement.

"Bard, come here," she hisses shakily. God, please don't let that thing outside hear her. It lumbers past the other set of windows, the night too dark to make out its shape, and Rowen swears she feels the ground shake. The glass that stands between them suddenly seems so fragile. If something that big were to throw its whole weight against it...

The shadow stops, head turning toward the cabin. Rowen can't move. She can't see its eyes, but the hair on her neck stands on end as if the creature is staring right at her.

Her shoulders hike to her ears before another instinct rushes through her body. Legs hot and shaky, she lunges, kneeing an end table and gathering Bard into her arms.

She doesn't look back out the windows, body vibrating as she slams the bedroom door behind them. Bard pants against her chest as she fumbles for the flashlight. Her knees are weak.

What should she *do*? She has to warn Asher. What if they're coming back and don't see —

Glass shatters beside her. Bard barks wildly as the flashlight spins across the floor, spraying horrifying shadows across the wall. Cold air hits her first, then warm breath as the beast snorts across her face.

Fifteen

Rowen

Someone is screaming. Rowen takes a breath and realizes it's *her*, one hand covering her head, her fingers brushing the furry animal as it claws its way inside.

The flashlight is across the room, pointed into the corner and leaving Rowen in the dark.

Then something else slams into the cabin, making the first animal yelp. Wood groans and snaps as the beast is dragged away, footfalls thundering as an animal roars into the darkness.

Frantically, Rowen scrambles for the flashlight. Bard is still in a frenzy, wriggling out of her arms as she tugs them both back into the living room. The wind slams the bedroom door shut behind her, sending her colliding with the wall.

They need to get upstairs. Nothing can get through those windows, right? Her breaths are short and shallow, flashlight jumping as she stumbles upstairs with Bard. He whines and trembles, licking at her arms before she brushes a trembling hand over his head. "It's ok. It's ok..."

It is not fucking ok. She sucks air through her nose, peering out a window for any sign of motion. Nothing else fights its way inside the lodge. There's only a trench dug through the snow, leading away from the bedroom and into the forest.

She has to find Asher. Trembling, she opens one of the guest rooms. "I have to go out, ok?" Maybe if she speaks to Bard, her voice will stop shaking. Maybe she'll convince herself to do what she has to. "I have to find Asher. I have to see if they're —"

Beneath her, the front door slams open. Asher's voice is sharp and desperate. "Rowen?!"

Relief floods her body. She presses a hand to her pounding heart as Bard races back down the stairs. She does her best to follow, leaning on the railing to keep her shaky legs beneath her. "Something happened. Something tried to get in —"

Asher closes the gap between them, tilting the flashlight up toward her face. "Are you hurt? Are you ok?" Their hands traverse her forehead, the curve of her cheek, the roundness of her jaw.

"I'm fine." She tries to settle into her body. "But the window is —" Then she catches a whiff of copper, her gaze dipping to Asher's bare chest. "Where's your coat?" she asks dazedly. There's a mark across Asher's pale skin. "Are you *bleeding*?"

Asher gives her face another once over before they're satisfied, moving toward the bathroom by the kitchen. "It's nothing."

Rowen follows with Bard underfoot. When Asher flicks the

bathroom light on, they try to block the mirror, but she gets a glimpse of maroon dripping from their left shoulder. "Oh my god, we need to get you —"

"It's fine." Quickly, Asher washes their hands, crouching to open the cabinet under the sink. "It looks worse than it is. It's just a scratch."

It's far from a scratch. The wounds are fresh and angry, yet Asher looks relieved at the sight, setting medicine on the counter as they run water over a washcloth.

Bard whines and paws at Asher's leg. They murmur sweetly to him, wincing at the rag pressed to the wound.

The fear in Rowen's body wanes, leaving her clammy and dizzy. This doesn't feel real. *Asher* doesn't feel real when she can't put her hands on them. Her voice is barely a whisper. "Are you sure?"

Asher holds her gaze in the mirror, as if they sense her panic. After a moment, they step back to make space. "See for yourself."

Her fingers curl around the doorjamb. Asher's never invited her into their space, not with so little between them. Carefully, she squeezes between Asher and the vanity, scrubbing her hands before she takes the rag. Their shoulder is firm under her touch, but she tries not to let her mind wander. Not to think about their bare skin and rising chest.

She moves on to the antiseptic. Asher tries not to show the sting, jaw tight as they stare down at Rowen's work. She's suddenly aware of how close they are, how Asher is wearing nothing but their thermal pants. How she's touching their bare chest.

Her fingers curl against their skin. "Where are your clothes?"

Asher's throat bobs, gaze tilting toward the door. "It gets hot working in the barn. I heard noise back here and just came running."

"Then how did you get this?"

They both look down to Asher's chest. Maybe that's a mistake. Cleaned up, the wounds don't look nearly as bad, but they're not a simple cut. Her hand slows, palm brushing Asher's chest. She's never seen them like this, long-healed scars under each of their pectorals. There are tattoos, too, markings scattered across their chest and arms. The symbols are simple, triangles and lines and circles in different combinations. What do they mean? The only marking with any detail is the stag skull spreading up their throat, antlers branching out across their neck...

And the patch of berries on their left pectoral. She almost couldn't make them out through the blood, but when she dabs it away, the berries are still vibrant and red. This tattoo is the only patch of color, collected in the almost-indistinguishable shape of an anatomical heart.

Are those...rowan berries? Her face heats, hand still pressed to their skin. Where the hell is her head at? She shouldn't be growing hot with Asher wounded in front of her, but they don't retract. They don't cover themself, letting Rowen's eyes traverse them, as if they're comfortable in this skin. As if they —

"You're staring," they whisper.

Her hand jerks away, elbow knocking the bottle of medicine into the sink. Her head ducks as she blushes. "I didn't mean — you just —" Her throat dries. God, they're so close. Their chest moves as they breathe, and her eyes cling to it.

She presses a hand to her cheek to will her flush away, and something else registers. "You're not cold."

Asher blinks when she lifts her head.

"You're not cold," she repeats, pressing her fingertips above their heart. Their skin is almost feverish. "You were outside in nearly nothing, but your skin isn't cold."

Rowen can't read their expression. They move her gently

out of the way, rummaging for bandages beneath the sink. "Yeah, I run hot."

"You didn't used to." She watches the muscles tense in their back. "You used to put your cold feet on my —"

"Things change." Asher grips the tops of the cabinet doors to stand. They tilt sideways, and Rowen's hand jerks out to steady them before they turn in the small space. "Sorry." Their face lingers before her, only a few inches of space between them. They're so close she can count their eyelashes as their gaze dips to her mouth. "I think I'm coming down. The adrenaline, you know..."

Rowen's teeth dig into her lip. "Should I wait to tell you about the window?"

The glossy look in Asher's eyes fades.

When they cross to the bedroom, Rowen prays nothing is waiting for them. Hopefully whatever that animal was hasn't returned. Asher pushes open the door and flicks on the light. "Goddammit."

It's worse than Rowen expected, glass shards scattered across the floor and bed. Other pieces hang in the window frame, but that's hardly the worst of the damage. Marks gouge into the wood around the window, like something was clawing its way in.

Worse still, the massive hole is letting in the cold. A sharp breeze flutters the curtains, and Rowen rubs her hands over her arms. "Two animals were fighting. It seemed like one was trying to get in. It sounded like —"

"A bear." Asher runs a hand through their hair. "At least, that's what I heard from outside."

The two of them stare at what's left of the window. Rowen can almost picture something reaching through, snatching Asher with its massive paw and dragging them into the forest.

"Whatever it was must have been disoriented." Asher steps over a piece of glass. "I'll set out some scent deterrents once it's light out."

Rowen's teeth chatter, and not just from the cold. "I don't think this is gonna work as a bedroom anymore."

Asher's teeth grit. "I'm sorry. This wasn't..." They shake their head.

"It's not *your* fault."

Asher doesn't reply. Eventually, they step back out of the room. "I'll hang a tarp and some blankets to keep the cold out. We can push a dresser in front of it too, to make sure nothing gets inside."

At least cleanup is a distraction. While Rowen sweeps the floor, Asher seals the hole. It keeps the room from being so cold, if nothing else. Then they strip the bed of its sheets. Aside from a light dusting of snow, the mattress is salvageable.

"I could squeeze it into one of the guest bedrooms, maybe." Asher runs a hand along their jaw as they inspect it. "Most of them are made for a Queen, max. And they've got other furniture in the way."

"We could move it into the living room," Rowen offers.

"I don't want to make you sleep out there."

She leans against the doorframe. "Does it really count as getting stranded if I don't have to use a makeshift bed?" A smile ticks on Asher's lips, and Rowen follows it. "We can keep a fire going to keep out any drafts, and the mattress is more than big enough for both of us." Before Asher can argue, she moves to the far side of the bed. "Come on: we can put a wall of pillows between us if you're so concerned."

After a long moment, Asher relents and tugs the mattress into the living room. It fits perfectly once they push the couch and coffee table back. By that time, the sun is rising over the top of the mountain, and Asher rubs blearily at their eyes. "I think we deserve some coffee."

Rowen looks over their handiwork with proud hands on her hips. So maybe she feels a little accomplished at getting

Asher to sleep on a real mattress. A bed big enough for the two of them, with Asher's warm body next to hers...

As Asher moves into the kitchen, their bare chest brushes her back. "Don't get any ideas."

But the dip in their voice inspires a hundred more.

Asher

Things are getting too fucking close.

After the...*moment* on the couch two nights ago, the Voice was inconsolable. It took the rest of that night to get it under control enough for Asher to stagger back to the lodge and leave Rowen a note. Just getting close to her stirred the creature to life again, which meant Asher had to drag themself back into the forest. They spent almost an entire twenty-four hours trying to wear the Voice out.

This season is the hardest they've ever had to fight it. The Voice grows stronger every December, but it's never been like *this*, as if Rowen's proximity calls it to the surface like a siren song.

In the kitchen now, Asher rests both hands on the counter,

head hanging as the coffee brews. It's exhausting keeping the Voice at bay, but it's even more tiring fighting off the forest animals. The bear in the window last night was a freak occurrence. Nothing like that has happened in years, not since Asher learned what the Wild Hunt entailed. Even from a distance, they recognized the sounds of glass breaking, a bear's roar, and Rowen's screams.

Asher didn't fight the Voice when it carried their body toward the lodge. For the first time, the two of them were in sync, one motivation pulsing through their body.

Get to Rowen.

It was a blur. By the time Asher's mind returned to them, they were barrelling through the front door in search of her. Asher's not sure what the Voice's motivations were. Has it softened toward Rowen? Or did it just not want some other creature snapping her in its jaws first?

Thank god Rowen hasn't pieced anything together, but time is ticking down. The Wild Hunt is drawing closer, stirring the animals into a frenzy they only find one night a year. Tomorrow night at sundown, Asher won't be able to stop any of it: the transformation, the feral creatures, the hunt hot on their heels.

Asher's jaw sets. The lake has to be frozen tomorrow; there is no other option. Rowen has to get off this mountain before anything else happens to her, and Asher will ensure she does.

When they pour the coffee, their wound throbs under the bandages, and not just from pain. They shut their eyes at the memory of Rowen's fingers brushing their bare chest for the first time.

It's not how they expected her to see them that way. Hell, they never expected her to see them again *at all*, except in silly fucking fantasies when their willpower was too weak. When the wind howled, and they pretended her body warmed the place next to them. When their thoughts were slurried with the scent of her hair, the softness of her skin, the scatter of her freckles...

Coffee splatters onto the counter. Asher curses and searches for a hand towel, but their thoughts are still distracted. When Rowen saw them bare for the first time, her face changed, but not the way they expected. Instead, her cheeks grew red, blending her freckles into one hot mass. Her lips parted. Her eyelids drooped.

Asher knows that look. They know *her* look. She wants them, not just the person they were ten years ago, but the person they are *now*.

Their stomach twists, but the knot pulls loose just as quickly. *This place has memories,* they remind themself. *She's stuck here. She doesn't know what you are now.*

The more you fight, the worse it gets.

Asher's tattoos sizzle. Deep inside, the Voice stirs awake at the mention of Rowen. Asher sets the pot back on the counter, thoughts sharp with lack of sleep. *What does that even mean? You only talk in riddles.*

You don't let anyone in because you think no one wants to be there. The Voice yawns. **We could have taken a bite of her by now, but no...**

In the living room, Bard's chin rests on Rowen's thigh as she scratches between his ears. Asher swallows and pulls their eyes away.

This is only hard because you make it hard.

Fury boils into Asher's thoughts. After days of torture, this is what the Voice brings them? After years of fighting to get their body back, this is all the Voice has to say? Asher's fingers curl around the edge of the counter.

This is hard *because I'm fucking possessed. Because my body's being held hostage. Because everything on this mountain is cursed, including me.* Venomous words swell inside them, poison with nowhere else to go. *If she knew about you — if anyone knew, they would run. No one wants this life. No one wants you. No one could ever want you, but some of us don't have a fucking choice!*

The words echo through their head and down through the rest of their body, as if there's nothing to stop the vibrations. As if Asher is hollow. As if the Voice has buried itself deep enough that it can't be reached or wounded. Asher's face burns, tongue suddenly heavy and clumsy.

"Is it ready?"

Asher nearly knocks the mugs to the floor when Rowen sidles up to the island behind them. A blanket is tucked around her shoulders, eyes bleary from lack of sleep. The sight digs into Asher's chest, far deeper than the wound on their shoulder. With a nod, they set the drink in front of her and turn back to grab their own. It feels too real, too *right* to have her here with them, curled up and cozy as if this cabin is an oasis instead of a prison.

Her voice is crusted with sleep. "I think we should get a tree."

Brows knit, Asher turns back to her. Surely they misheard. Rowen's sweater sleeves cover both her hands, curled around her mug as her perfect lips blow away steam.

All Asher can do is stare. When she lifts her brows, Asher clears their throat. "Get a tree?"

Rowen nods. "A Christmas tree. We should cut one down and bring it in." Her eyes focus on the dark pool of her drink. "There's plenty of selection. It's not like anyone's going to miss it."

Asher is certain their eyebrows are lifted to their hairline. The girl must have lost her mind, still delirious from the scare. They hardly know how to respond. "I told you, it's dangerous. The animals —"

"— have already broken into the cabin." Rowen sets her coffee down, inhaling slowly through her nose before she continues. "Look, I can't spend another day cooped up in here. Not after last night. I'll be petrified of every little sound while you run off to — wherever you go." Her hand waves toward the barn. "I need a distraction. I've been stuck in here for days trying to entertain myself. If animals are busting through the windows, I think a fifteen-minute trip outside is safe enough."

Anxiety branches through Asher's throat. "It's not —"

"Asher..." Rowen settles her hands on the island before she lifts her gaze. It's more certain than Asher expects, as if she's prepared for this moment, a flash of Wild Rowen straightening her shoulders. "I'm not asking your permission. I'm telling you what I'm going to do, and I'm offering for you to come with me."

Asher is stunned into silence. Rowen looks tempted to squirm in discomfort, but she keeps herself still, letting the silence settle between them. It's been years since Asher saw this look on her face: steady and certain, not bending to someone else's whims. Despite the circumstance, Asher can't help but feel a little proud.

Outside the window, there's no sign of any other haunted creatures approaching. Maybe last night scared them off for a few hours, even more than Asher's presence normally does. This is probably the best chance they'll have to slip in and out of the cabin, and if Rowen's determined to go either way...

With a smile, Asher mutters into their cup. "What better time to operate dangerous machinery than with no sleep?"

Within the next half hour, they're both bundled up and trudging through the snow with their equipment. "Straight to the hillside with the trees," Asher reiterates. "We're not going near the forest." Nerves snap at Asher's heels, their head swiveling for any cursed creatures scurrying closer. The animals keep their distance. There are no warbling birds or chittering squirrels, as if the entire mountain is watching from afar.

Asher can't blame it. Even with the rifle on their back, Rowen is a distraction from their vigilance. Her gaze does dart apprehensively toward the woods, but with every step, color blooms in her face as she tilts it toward the sun. Out here, she blossoms like the return of spring, an image Asher had long-forgotten.

She blooms like Wild Rowen, a flower growing determinedly from harsh earth. She is not curated perfection here. On the mountain, nothing hides the dark circles under her eyes. Her hair whips around her face, nose pink as she moves through the snow. Among the trees and hills and peaks rising up around them, she is small...yet she's the only thing that draws Asher's eyes. Looking at her, they can almost pretend there's nothing else. No mountain. No curse. Just —

"Don't tell me the coffee didn't help." Rowen waves a gloved hand to get their attention. "Do I need to operate the chainsaw?"

Laughter puffs from their mouth, belying the ache in their chest. As Rowen peers out over the sloping hill of trees, Asher warns, "Pick something small."

After a moment of consideration, she points to an impossibly massive tree at the bottom of the hill. It's at least twice the size of the lodge. "That'll do nicely."

Asher gestures to a scraggly thing nearby. "This one, you said?" It's more of a root than a tree, wilting like it's straight out of a Christmas special.

Instead of arguing, Rowen's lip juts out. "It does look like it needs a good home. Someone to take care of it."

Asher's eyes roll. "I was *joking.* We can get you something better than that."

But Rowen gingerly straightens the tree, supporting its measly weight to keep it upright. "It looks lonely."

"It's a *tree.*"

Eventually, they compromise, loading a full-size tree onto

the sled as Rowen carries the dinky tree against her chest. Back at the lodge, they finagle the thick tree inside with Bard yapping happily. Their tree leans only slightly against the stairs, so Rowen sets her little one next to it. It can't keep itself upright, but when she rests it against the other, it's almost passable.

"Cheater," Asher mutters as she steps back to admire their work.

She nudges their hip with hers. "Remember when Mrs. Norling let you pick the first tree of the season?"

The long-forgotten memory surfaces like a fish through water, hooking a smile onto Asher's face. "I picked the closest tree to the lodge. I don't think it was even four feet tall."

"She was *not* impressed." Rowen swaggers past them, spinning on her heel. "Lucky you had *me* to suggest we put it in the staff cabins. Look at us, starting Christmas traditions."

Her smile is warm and soft. Asher's stomach knots, a thought darting through their mind before they can stop it. *This could be our new tradition.*

Rowen turns to one of the plastic tubs, her eyes brightening. "Do you think the old tree decorations are in the attic too?"

Asher shrugs. "Maybe: I left most of that stuff alone. Couldn't be bothered to move it." The lie creeps up the back of Asher's neck. The truth is that they couldn't handle digging through old memories and encountering Rowen: her handwriting, her craftsmanship, her touch.

And now the girl herself is here, overwhelming Asher in ways nothing else ever could.

She tucks her hands into her pockets. "Maybe we can decorate later. After dark, like we used to."

Under her gaze, Asher's skin heats. "I guess I could get some work done —"

"No." The word seems to surprise her, shy smile growing

as she savors the "no" like a delicacy she hasn't tasted in ages. "Stay with me. We can do some other traditions...for old time's sake."

Her mouth presses into a pleading line, waiting for their answer — waiting for them to deny her again. On the couch, Bard's ears perk, eagerly awaiting Asher's answers.

They shouldn't. They should put the wall back up between them and Rowen, find a safe distance and maintain it, stop themself from pretending this is something it can't be. But that gaping pit inside them spreads, as if it can get close enough to reach Rowen.

Asher tugs off their coat. "I'm not baking cookies."

Seventeen

Asher

They bake cookies.

The legs on Asher's reindeer are comically thin, but Asher can't seem to mind when it makes Rowen giggle. There's no telling how long the powdered sugar has been in the back of the pantry, so they eat the cookies without icing to be safe. Rowen even manages to find holiday onesies in the tubs, which Asher refuses, but the way the fabric clings to her curves has them second-guessing. Somehow, she also finds the only remaining Christmas movies in the place, tucked into one of the attic tubs. Despite Asher's grumbling, they both watch them all, curled up close but not-too-close on the couch. Beneath the blanket, Asher brushes Rowen's leg. She's as warm as they remember. Asher tries to find something to be dour about, but even holiday magic is fun with her. If nothing else, Asher gets to complain about the logistics of Santa's sleigh, and Rowen gets to chide them to believe in something.

Brick by brick, the wall Asher erected between them begins to crumble.

Before they know it, the sun is long-gone behind the trees. Soup is the only reasonable answer for dinner, and Rowen has no trouble finding her cutting board and knife as Asher starts the pot on the stove.

It's easy being together. That thought sneaks into Asher's mind, so smooth and quiet that it startles them. How can it be this easy after so long of being impossible?

They still don't have an answer when they finish dinner, washing and drying dishes next to each other. There's still no answer when she convinces them to let her make a batch of hot cider. As she does, they maneuver decor tubs down from the attic and wrap the tree in lights.

Once Rowen brings the steaming cups into the living room, she peels the lid off one of the tubs with a gasp. "I can't believe Mrs. Norling kept this..."

Delicately, she pulls out a mangled star. Clearly, no one else has handled the piece this gingerly, its paint scuffed and points bent as light passes through missing panes of color. Dried glue peeks out from the seams, yet even in its ragged state, it fills Asher with nostalgia. "Why wouldn't she throw it out?" they marvel. "That thing was broken for *years*."

"Do you remember the first time it broke?" Rowen holds the star to her chest as she drags a step-stool toward the tree. "The *actual* first time, not the coverup."

Asher's brows knit. "The family of squirrels, right? They were burrowed inside the tree when we brought it in?"

"No!" Rowen gasps, eyes sparkling. "I can't believe I get to tell you this." She steps onto the stool, but it brings her nowhere near the top of the tree. She doesn't notice. "No,

Asher, it was *John Michael.*"

Asher's mouth drops open in shock. "'Parking spot asshole' John Michael? The guy who insisted on playing Santa, even though he had none of the jelly *or* jolly?"

Rowen can't contain her laughter. "I swear! He was mad someone else put the star on before he got to. Matter of fact…" Her brows knit, fingernails tapping the star before she chuckles. "I think it was *you.*"

Asher scoffs playfully. "I just wanted to get it over with! The first night of the season is always all that fucking decorating." A fizzy feeling spreads through them at the memory. That was also the first night they met Rowen. The first night she caught them staring. The first night Asher was so distracted, they picked up whatever decoration they could find and stuck it to the tree.

"Well," her voice dips into a brief John Michael impression, "you stole his honor as the most senior member of staff."

From the grin on her face, Asher can't bring themself to regret it.

She tucks hair behind her ear, painting a vivid picture as she gestures. "So the night it happened, everyone else went back to the staff cabins. I was still stocking linens, so John Michael didn't see me when he went to the top of the stairs — oh, right." She steps down from the stool and makes her way up the steps. "He went to take the star off and place it back on, you know, for the ceremony of it. For the *principle.*" She mimics the motion, setting the star ever-so-gently on top of the tree. "But he dropped it! Straight to the floor from the second story. It scattered everywhere, and he was just — *staring* at it."

Asher leans against the railing, trying to reconcile it. "But the next day, there was squirrel poop all over the floor. A hole in the tree trunk. I mean, fuck, there were acorns!"

"He staged the scene! I don't know how he came up with

it. One second he was standing at the top of the stairs, then he just ran out into the snow..." The image makes her dissolve into laughter as she gasps around the words. "He was digging — for acorns in his bare feet. I could see him from the window. Then he took — his little pocket knife — and started sawing a hole in the Christmas tree..." Her joy is infectious, making Asher's face ache from the smile straining their cheeks. *That* makes Rowen laugh harder, tears escaping as she sinks to the floor. "And he rolled — chocolate chips — to make them look like poop!"

Her laughter is so strong that it becomes silent, open-mouthed joy as her shoulders shake. She's giddy and sleep-deprived, beguiling Asher. No matter how they try to settle themself, amusement sneaks into their voice. "Why didn't you say anything?! At least to *me*. We told the squirrel story to new people every year!"

"Because it was a hit!" Rowen blinks tears away, leaning back against the bannister. "Everybody loved telling that story. I think Mrs. Norling liked it even more than the star."

Softness settles onto Asher's face. Of course: Rowen let them keep the story because it made them happy. Because that's what Rowen does for other people.

After a few deep breaths, her laughter settles into a few errant giggles. Firelight reflects off the star, beautiful in its tragedy. She stares wistfully up at it. "Besides, I couldn't tell you. You and I weren't...close yet."

Close. That singular word feels blissfully, impossibly right as they watch her at the top of the staircase. After years of chasing off the painful memories of this cabin, here they are making new ones. Asher won't be able to look at this room without seeing her there, the scent of cookies and cider lingering in the air. No matter how Asher tried to keep this place barren and cold, it's gleaming after only a few days under Rowen's care.

They have to look away, to look anywhere else, turning

back to the box of ornaments. "Shit, Norling really did keep everything."

Rowen moves back down the stairs, following Asher's gaze and retrieving the ornament by its twine. It's a shoddily assembled sled, made of twigs and popsicle sticks. "I remember this day." She hangs the ornament gently from one of the branches. "If I recall, *I* beat *you*."

Asher snorts. "On a technicality."

"*Yeah*," she calls over her shoulder, "that's how they judge races."

"I still call bullshit." As expected, Rowen gasps. Asher grins cheekily. "You didn't finish the race with your sled; you finished with *mine*. That has to be a disqualification."

"It doesn't matter which *sled* crosses the finish line first!" Rowen holds up a finger. "It matters which *person*."

"You only crossed first because you were on top of me!"

"Because you ran into me pulling my sled out of the woods!" Rowen gapes. "I could have *died*."

"Oh, please." Asher's eyes roll fondly. "I caught you. You were never in any danger."

"You're lucky I only wanted first place." Tauntingly, Rowen steps into their space. "I could have taken you to the cleaners. All of this..." She gestures to the lodge around them before she presses a finger to Asher's chest, careful to avoid their wound. "Could be mine."

Her body's close, putting off more heat than the fire — or maybe that's in Asher's head. Their gaze dips to the proud curve of her smile, and they can't help but match it. "You can have it."

Rowen's face shifts uncertainly. It takes a moment for Asher's words to play back in their ears. Fuck. They hadn't meant — however it sounded. Like a proposition. An offer.

Asher clears their throat, reaching into the box and pulling out the first thing they find. Their fingers curl over it protectively, raised texture pressed against their skin. They can't bring themself to look at it, tracing the ceramic heart with the tips of their fingers. If not for the ornament's shape, the white lace pattern could almost pass for a snowflake, like any other Christmas decor.

Sweat pricks on Asher's back, torn between two impulses — shatter the ornament in the fire or hold it so close that it embeds into their chest.

At their silence, Rowen peers down at their hand. The air in the room stills. Asher's mind fires rapidly, unsure how to proceed, but Rowen takes the heart gently from them. "I can't believe it's still in one piece."

The delicate heart took the two of them all four seasons to pull off. The ornament still isn't perfect, but they poured all their skill into it after weeks helping families make their own pieces out of clay. This heart was the first and only thing that Asher and Rowen made together, the only evidence that the two of them took up the same space. Both their hands touched this thing, carving their names into it the same way Rowen carved herself into Asher's very being.

She turns the piece in her hand, tracing her fingers over the two names interlocked on the back, as if that sight is more breathtaking than the finish on the front. "Sorry..." Shaking her head, she closes her fingers, lifting her gaze back to theirs. "We can get rid of it. It's not your name..."

"We should keep it." And they mean it, even if their smile is tight for a completely different reason. "I got a scar on my leg for that."

A wet laugh slips out of Rowen as she clutches the ornament. "That's right. It burned your leg hair off." When she turns back to the tree, she searches its many boughs and branches before she hangs their ornament on the only strong limb of her scraggly little one. When she steps back, they both admire it.

"It's a shame you never liked Christmas," she whispers.

Asher digs their teeth into their lip. "I did like Christmas...for a few years."

Puzzled, Rowen tilts her head toward them. "When was that?"

They don't answer, throat straining from all the words fighting for a place on their tongue. *When I was here with you. When nothing else mattered. When you weren't ashamed of us. Of me.* Every good memory they have of this place is because of Rowen, and when she left, Asher could no longer remember why they'd ever enjoyed anything.

Rowen's lips part as if she understands, and it burns like the kiln all over again. Asher's hungry for the pain, desperate to be fired under Rowen's gaze. They want to change their history and uproot everything that happened since Rowen left. They want to take the clay of their life between their hands, squeezing and forming it into something else.

But that clay has long dried. There's no molding or reshaping it; the only change left would be for it to shatter.

It doesn't matter what Rowen brings to this place now; she will not be here forever. She *can't*. She is not a cursed thing. She has a life outside of here, people she's never learned to say "no" to, a world she's constantly pleasing at the cost of herself.

And Asher is not the same as they were before. They're not the person she cared for. They're different and dangerous and damned, just like everything else on this mountain.

Asher turns their back on the tree...and her. "I'm gonna turn in early." Before she can speak, they lay the bricks back into the wall between them. "I'm just...fucking tired. You can stay up and decorate, or read, or whatever. It won't keep me awake."

But that's a lie. They won't sleep for hours yet, but they can pretend. It's better than acting like they can look at her and not feel everything. Head down, they strip to their underclothes, settling onto one side of the mattress.

For the first time, they realize the Voice has not returned.

Letter #26

It's been nine years since we last spoke, and here I am, still writing to you.

My boyfriend called me "princess" today. I broke up with him. How could I explain it's because that name belongs to you? No matter how much time passes, it's still yours, even after all these years.

Do you want me to be honest? Of course you do. That's what you always said.

I'm pissed. I'm pissed at you. I'm pissed at a lot of things, and I know I can never put words to it in person, but — FUCK! I'd rather be pissed than keep missing you. I'd rather be pissed than cry about how we never got to see what this could have been.

Maybe it would have been nothing, but...no. It was never nothing. It was always going to be something. But maybe it would have ended anyway, and I'll never know that, because you just disappeared.

That's the worst part: the not-knowing. Doesn't it bother you? Do you ever think about me? Do you know I've spent so much time looking for you? I know you didn't like being "on the grid" or whatever, but it's like you fell off the face of the earth after that night.

I hope you're still out there, even if you're avoiding me. I can't deal with the alternative.

I feel like I lost my voice since I lost you. I recognize it, but it's hard to stop worrying about everyone's opinions when they prefer me catering to them. You were the only person I could be myself around, and look how that turned out. Better for me to keep making other people happy, because at least then one of us is.

You never cared about pleasing other people, but I don't think you cared about pleasing yourself, either. You didn't feel like you deserved it, did you? But you did. You always did.

Do you think you were too busy hating yourself to see that I was trying to love you? Were you protecting yourself from the world, or were you just keeping yourself from me?

I won't stop missing you. I know that. The anger will fade, but you will go back to being the wound in me that never heals.

— R.

Eighteen

Asher

Asher can't find Rowen in the dark.

They stumble through the snow, trying to follow tracks
that are quickly covered by swirling flakes. It's impossible, but
they have to try. They have to —

Rowen's scream makes Asher's heart flutter like a trapped
bird. She has to be nearby. They have to find her. Pushing up
from the ground, they stagger toward her voice until it's tossed
by the wind. Now her cries echo off a rock wall, then the cluster
of trees, then back in the direction they came.

Asher can't follow the sound. They shout her name, but
everything is muffled by snow.

A nauseating crunch breaks above the wind — then
silence. Asher's entire body vibrates, as if a growl emanates
from the earth. They shoulder deeper into the forest, shoving

branches aside as trees cling to their clothes.

A new smell hits their nose, tinny and sharp, making their stomach roil as they tear through the trees. Frozen roots catch their boots as if the forest itself is holding them back. Bark draws blood from their palms, but they keep pushing and pushing until they tumble into a clearing.

Everything stops. There is no wind, no falling snow, no sound except their panicked pulse and ragged breathing. One column of moonlight beams through the trees, illuminating untouched snow before something dark seeps across it. A trickle becomes a stream, then a river, an ocean of darkness tinged with red.

Asher crawls through the snow. There is no sign of Rowen's broken form, but something else waits in the shadows. Its furred body is as thick as a tree trunk, antlers spread like branches and casting Asher into darkness. The creature's tongue laves over its fangs, blood dripping from its snout onto a canvas of cold white.

Asher's voice breaks. "You killed her."

"I consumed her," the creature rumbles.

Asher's going to be sick. The Voice has been silent for hours, returning only to do *this*. "I knew you would." Asher's bare fingers curl in the snow, stinging with pain as their stomach heaves. "I *knew* you would."

The Voice is unruffled. "She gave herself to me."

"She would never do that!" Asher screams. Who would give themself willingly to this *thing*? Bile rises in Asher's throat. "You're sick. You're a monster."

The beast tilts its head, blinking the dark pools of its eyes. "I am you."

Asher clenches their own shut. "No, you're not, you're —"

The Voice maintains the same even cadence. "The more you fight, the worse it gets."

"What does that *mean*?!" Asher shouts. "Tell me what you

mean! Tell me what you want!"

The beast surges forward, slamming its head against Asher's like two bucks warring in the forest. "That's not how the magic works!" the beast snarls. "You called to me, and I answered. Now the mountain is calling to you."

Gritting their teeth, Asher presses back against the creature with all their might. The beast snorts, pawing the ground to keep its footing.

"I've told you what is needed," the beast rumbles.

"What *you* need."

"What *we* need!" Pain sears through Asher's skull when the beast surges forward. "Now bring it to me!"

Asher lurches up in bed, straining against a force that's no longer there. Two soft hands hold their cheeks, bringing Rowen's concerned eyes into focus. They search her body for wounds, but even in the dim light, they know there's nothing.

"It was dream," she breathes. "It was a dream. You're ok..."

They are back on the mattress in the living room, lit only by the fireplace and glowing tree. Outside, the mountain is quiet, barely even a whisper of wind. In the kitchen, Bard settles back into his bed. No creatures roam near the cabin, yet Asher's body is still covered in sweat. They set their feet on the ground, tugging their damp shirt overhead as they rise from the mattress.

"Where are you going?" Rowen asks, as if she knows the answer.

Asher swallows the guilt. "Might as well get some work done. I won't get back to sleep." They dab their chest with the t-shirt. "You should, though. I didn't mean to wake you..."

Their voice trails off. In front of the tree, Rowen looks...magical. Hair curls around her shoulders, eyelids heavy above the freckles on her face. It takes a moment for Asher to realize she's looking at them the same way — sweat glistening on their chest, hair mussed, voice thick with sleep.

It coils tight in Asher's stomach, and they toss their shirt aside, too warm now to do any good.

Rowen crosses her legs. "Do you want me to pet your hair?" Asher scoffs at the absurdity, but she doesn't back down. "*Excuse me*, but it always worked on you. Don't act like you're too big and bad for it now."

Asher can't help but smile. There's Wild Rowen again, too disoriented from the sudden waking to bite her tongue. She doesn't roll over at Asher's gruffness, because she knows when they're being surly for the sake of it.

They know how they *should* answer her. They should go out to the barn and put some respectable distance between the two of them. Hell, Asher could at least busy themself in the kitchen...but Rowen's right. It's been years since anyone played with their hair. Cautiously, Asher sinks back onto the mattress. "Just for a minute."

Rowen beams, moving to the head of the bed and settling Asher's pillow into her lap. They glare at her attempt to pamper them. "It's a better angle!" she insists. With a sigh, Asher lays on their side, and Rowen's hands move into their hair.

Asher tries not to tense as she combs through the dark curls, massaging her nails into their scalp. Before long, their body grows heavy again.

"Your hair is softer than I remember," she murmurs. "What do you use on it? Mountain dirt and spring water?"

A moony smile crosses their lips. "Just dirt." It's all they can do to keep their voice from spiraling into a moan. Rowen has not lost any of her skill, fingers dragging gently through the strands. Jealousy gnaws at Asher's chest, but they keep their voice as light as they can manage. "You must have done this with a lot of people over the years."

Rowen's hand slows. Asher swallows, but they force their expression to stay neutral. It's a fair question, since she asked about their history the first night at dinner. After a moment, Rowen returns to her previous pace. "Not really."

"Oh, come on," Asher hums. "Gorgeous girl like you...you had a winter fling. Surely there were summer boys to keep you company." *Boys*. The word is intentional, but Asher doesn't feel any braver for saying it.

They force themself still. Rowen's nails scrape the back of their neck, lifting their hair on end before she whispers, "I thought about *you* every summer."

The coil ratchets tighter in Asher's gut. They try not to think about how their head rests in her lap, so close to the warmth of her thighs. "Yeah, right."

Her motions are pointed now, tugging at the base of their hair before she loosens her hold again. "We always wore a lot of layers up here on the farm." Her voice is dreamy, but the solid grip of her hand makes Asher's stomach twist. "I always wondered what you looked like in a bathing suit. Water dripping off your skin, glowing under the sun..."

Her nails drag against their scalp, so deep a groan slips through Asher's lips.

There's a husky smile in her voice. "That good, huh?"

They stretch against the pillow, burrowing deeper between her thighs. When they rock the top of their head against her, her hand stutters.

"It's *alright*," Asher taunts smugly. "Maybe I am too big and bad for it now."

A gasp escapes them as Rowen's fingers tug the hair at the nape of their neck, drawing their head back. Their throat is arched and exposed, flushing under her gaze.

With a growing smirk, she leans closer. "Sort that attitude out before I sort it for you."

The coil in Asher's stomach springs. Rowen's eyes widen as if she senses it, but she's helpless to stop them rolling her beneath them. Both their chests heave, eyes locked as Asher pins Rowen's wrists above her head.

She was only teasing, but Asher has shot past playing games. Her pupils are blown, hair splayed across the sheets — *their* sheets on *their* bed in *their* cabin. Her full lips part, flustered as she tries to squeeze her thighs together around one of theirs.

Both their breaths are heavy in the silence. It feels like a tipping point, like they're balanced on a ledge and unsure which way to fall — back into shallow propriety, or down into something so much deeper.

Rowen sees the warring thoughts in their head. "Make the most of our few days, right?" Wantonly, her voice trembles. "Then we go back to our lives, no matter what happens here."

It sparks pain and passion in equal measure. Asher knows there's no going back from this — not for them. They used to label the years "Before Rowen" and "After Rowen," but that was never really the truth. There has never been an "after" her. She lingers in every crevice of their being, no matter how they try to keep her out. There is only "With Rowen" and "Without Rowen," and the only difference is how much the thought of her wounds them.

"No one else knows what a wild thing you are, do they?" Asher pants. Rowen fights their hold, teeth digging into her lip as her body arches. Asher is captivated by her twitches and squirms, like a little creature about to be devoured. "Out there, you're a perfect little princess. You wear the right clothes and bow your head and do whatever the world tells you. You never cop an attitude. You never put anyone out. You never *need* anything...but not here." When Asher nudges their knee between her legs, she whimpers, and Asher salivates. "No, *here*, you pull my hair. You make demands. You sit on my lap and tell me to be mean before you use my leg to make yourself come." Their fingers spread over her wrists. "What happened to that sweet little facade, Ro?"

Her lip wobbles when she grinds against their leg. She can't help it. Just like Asher can't help the flare of arousal at this version of Rowen that no one else gets. Asher gets the truth, the *real* parts, the desire she denies.

And Asher would never discard any of them. Just like Rowen has never discarded any of them, peeling off their pointed exterior to set her mouth against the soft parts beneath.

She knows it, too. Her voice is barely a whisper. "You don't scare me."

Asher's abdomen clenches. They need to stop this. They need to pull away, to move off the bed, to sleep on the fucking floor as long as it keeps them from being sucked into something hopeless.

But Rowen looks up at them like they mean something, like this is more than what it is, and Asher is a glutton for punishment — for Rowen — if nothing else.

"I should." They circle their knee between her legs. "You should be very fucking scared, princess, because there's no coming back from this." When they lower their mouth to her ear, she shudders at the teeth dragging against the lobe. "When you go back to the real world, it won't satisfy you. You'll have to wear that precious mask again, but you're gonna wish you were still here getting fucked on worn sheets in the middle of the living room. You're gonna wish you were still stuck in this cabin in the woods. You're gonna wish it was *me* wearing out your pretty little clit instead of you and your memories."

Rowen whimpers, desperate for friction, but Asher holds themself back. Their body is hard and hot, straining against their skin as if they want to be free of it. As if they aren't close enough to her. They drag their tongue over her throat, lapping up the vibration of her gasp when she speaks: "I want you to fuck my mouth."

Asher's weight falters, heading swimming. Where did that

come from? Why is she thinking about that?

"Please." Her throat is taut, scraping their mouth. "I know we never did before, but *please*, if you'll let me…"

A hiss escapes Asher, their hair brushing her shoulder as their head hangs. Everything in them aches at the thought of her pink mouth smearing against them, her pretty moans buzzing against their body as her big eyes look up at them —

Rowen's already a mess, rutting against their knee with a pitiful hitch in her voice, as if the thought affects her as much as Asher. "We don't have to. But after the bathroom, I thought maybe — if you'd like it…"

"Ok," they pant, fighting not to let desire overtake them. Thoughts pummel against their skull. *Yes, I would like it. Yes, I've dreamed about it over and over. Yes, I need to feel you like that so badly.* "But there are rules."

Asher

Rowen stills immediately, obedient and willing to do exactly as Asher asks.

They know they don't have to do this. If they denied her, she would accept it without question...but they don't want to deny her. They want to *feel it*. They want this, the thing they've spent a decade picturing. They want to give them both what Asher has denied themself.

"Only put your mouth on my — clit," Asher instructs. "And don't use your hands."

Rowen nods ardently, eyes locked on theirs as if she wants nothing more than to please them. It sends a hot shiver down their spine.

"And don't call it anything. Don't use any terminology,

just..." Already, Asher feels themself pulling away from their body and out of this moment. *No.* They try to shake themself out of it. They don't want to disassociate; they want to be here, they want to do *this*...

Above her head, Rowen tightens her fingers around theirs to bring them back. "What if you tie my hands behind me, and fuck my mouth so I can't talk?"

Weight settles back into Asher's body as they groan, releasing her with a nod. "Get on the floor."

She follows without question, sinking to her knees beside the mattress. In one of the decor tubs, Asher finds an unopened pack of bows and ribbons. They circle behind her before they crouch, brushing their mouth against her ear.

"Give me your hands." She shivers, crossing her wrists at the small of her back as Asher knots a thick, red ribbon around them. "Can you get out?"

She twists her shoulders and elbows, but the binding stays put. God, she looks like a fucking present, the bow situated above her perfect ass. Asher trails their fingers against her palm, and she squeezes back.

"Say the safeword, and the ribbon comes off," they murmur.

She follows them with her eyes. "And you say the word if you want to stop."

Asher sinks down on the mattress with their knees open. With Rowen's hands tied, she's at their mercy. Once she leans forward, the only way to keep her balance will be pressing her mouth against them. Arousal and nerves swarm in tandem in Asher's stomach as they part the opening in the front of their boxer briefs.

It's dark enough they aren't completely exposed, but Rowen's eyes sparkle like it's Christmas morning. Eagerly, she opens her mouth and leans forward, but Asher grabs her hair to keep her in place.

"You wait," they command, "until I give it to you. Until you ask nicely enough."

The voice that comes out of them is more powerful and controlled than they feel. It makes them settle into their body, as if they're the prize Rowen acts like they are. Asher's already swollen from her eagerness, but they want to make her wait. To make her *beg*.

When they don't move her any closer, her eyes flit up to theirs. At the sight of their cruel smirk, she whimpers. "Please..." Her legs tighten together, hips rocking where she sits on her knees. It's not an act. She wants them, *truly* wants them, like she's been just as deprived of this, too.

Asher still doesn't move, cupping her cheek with their other hand.

She makes a broken sound. "*Please*, Ash —"

Their hand tightens in her hair. "God —*fuck*." She's never said *this* name like that, torn through with desire, desperate and needy. It's not even their full first name, but Asher's already burning with want from the first syllable. It's too good. It's *too fucking good*, and it's going to their head, unwinding the restraints on the reckless creature inside them. "You want to be my little toy?"

Rowen nods hopelessly, mouth open and watering.

Asher tightens their hold. "You want to be my little plaything that I rip out of the wrapping?" They gather her hair behind her neck, as if the sight of her like this isn't driving them mad. "Want me to leave you under the tree all tied up? Put a pretty bow in your hair while you wait for me to play with you?"

Needy tears form in Rowen's eyes, her thighs clenching for any semblance of friction.

"Say it," Asher demands. "Tell me you're my little fucktoy."

The words are a mess in her mouth, breathless and pitiful. "I'm your little fucktoy. Play with me, *use me*, however you want, just *please...*"

"What?" Asher drags their thumb down Rowen's bottom lip. "What does my little doll want me to do with her? 'Please' what?"

Her lip quivers. "Please fuck my face."

And Asher finally, *finally* does.

Easing Rowen forward by her hair, they guide her mouth between their legs. Her eyes roll back as she moans with relief, like *she's* the one getting sucked off. She does exactly as she's told, keeping her hot mouth only on their clit, flicking her tongue like she knows how.

Asher's head tips back as their hips roll. Arousal coats them like armor, drawing a breathy laugh from them. "Who taught you to give head like this?"

A little smirk plays on her lips, making Asher groan. She pulls back enough to speak against them. "All those winters here, I had a *very* good teacher."

Asher's abs flex as they hold Rowen in place. This is so much better than the fantasies. Their mind could never have conjured exactly how beautiful she looks, how wet and warm her mouth is, how eagerly she performs.

When she hollows her cheeks again, it almost looks like Asher's fucking a cock between her lips. Then Rowen presses the tip of her tongue to the roof of her mouth, giving their clit something to nudge against, like they're fucking the back of her throat.

Asher could combust, but they don't want this to end — not yet. They pull her off of them and up to their lips, licking their taste out of her mouth. "What if we play with another toy?"

Her tongue curls against theirs, her head bobbing before they move toward the hall closet and retrieve a small backpack.

A little laugh escapes her. "You keep that out here?"

Her humor is gone when Asher pulls the dildo from the

bag. Now *that's* the desired effect, her eyelids drooping as she clenches her thighs together. Asher smirks as they adjust themself into the boxer brief harness. "I had to move it once *someone* started sleeping in my room." They slot the toy into place, letting the heavy head dip. "But I can put it away, if you don't think you can handle it."

"Do not," Rowen sucks in a breath, "fucking *dare*."

Asher approaches her, holding their flesh-colored toy against them. When Asher and Rowen were younger, there was no time or privacy for anything but their bodies. They made do with mouths and legs and hands, but Asher spent years wondering what the two of them could get up to now. With experience and toys and a space all to themselves...

Rowen looks ready to take it all, teeth scraping her lip. "Do you have a word you want me to call this?"

Asher flinches. They know what they *want* her to call it, but the thought of saying it aloud makes them cringe. With a swallow, they shrug.

Rowen keeps her eyes on theirs. "Do you want me to call it your strap? Or your dick?"

The word zings straight to Asher's gut, their fingers tightening around the toy's base.

Rowen's brows lift, lips barely brushing the head of the toy. "Your cock?"

A groan breaks through Asher's lips, voice rasping. "Yeah, those two."

Rowen looks up at them from beneath her lashes. Head radiates through Asher's body as she lifts on her knees, turning those sinful eyes up toward them while her mouth curls around the words. "I want your dick in my mouth."

Asher grits their teeth, hips rocking forward. When *she* says it, it doesn't sound awkward or uncertain; it sounds unbelievably sexy. With her on her knees, tongue swiping the end of the toy, Asher swears they can feel it.

Luxuriously, Rowen licks over the head and meets their eyes. "I want your cock on my tongue."

That's fucking *it*. Asher doesn't make her wait any longer, tapping against her lips. "Then open up."

Immediately, she lays out the flat of her tongue for Asher to sink into her mouth. They reach the back of her throat, shifting their hips as her lips stretch around them. With every thrust, their cock grows wet and slick, coated in her spit as she swallows them back. God, they could fuck her like this for hours, doing nothing but relishing her sloppy sounds.

But they need to be so much deeper, to fill her like they've never had the chance to. With one hand in her hair, they pull her to her feet, smirking at the disappointed sound she makes. Her lips search for Asher's mouth, but they don't give it to her.

"Since you thought of me every summer..." Their other hand travels down the front of her onesie, unsnapping each button until they can get their hand against her cunt. She gasps, rising on her toes, hands still trapped behind her back. The fabric clings to her curves, barely concealing her breasts now that Asher's stripping her down. "Why don't you tell me all the other times you thought about me? How I haunted you?" Because god knows she's still haunting them. They circle her clit, hissing at the wetness as they sink a finger inside. "Let's take a walk down memory lane, princess."

Twenty

Rowen

It's only Asher's body that keeps Rowen upright. The two of them have never been this close. Asher's never let her see them like this, stripped down and bare with their skin pressed against hers.

They keep her close, their fingers finding the ribbon behind her back. With one hand, they unravel the knot, never removing their eyes from hers. Her legs tremble. How do they know how to do this? How do they move with such certainty, a wicked glint in their eye, filling up every inch of their skin? This is not the Asher who consumed her world before. That was only a piece of them, the rest buried beneath the surface. This Asher is more of themself, breaking through the crust she used to know and flowing over her.

It makes her head spin. Tentatively, she presses her hands between their chests, dragging her nails down their stomach. It makes them hold her tighter. Asher is so *warm*, hot from the nightmare or the fire or desire.

Their fingers lift her chin and her attention. She wants to kiss them. She *needs* to, but they make her whine instead as their mouth draws closer.

"Tell me," they repeat, lips brushing hers, "how else you thought about me."

Arousal slices deep in her stomach. Her lips tremble, cheeks growing hot under the spotlight of their gaze. What hasn't she imagined? Since the year they met, her wanton mind has wandered over the ways she might have them. Any moment Rowen could be alone, Asher arrested her thoughts. She hid her desires behind sunglasses, in the pages of books, behind the shower door.

"I thought about you," she breathes, "when I worked at summer camp. I thought about what it'd be like if you worked there, too. If you'd make bracelets with me at Arts & Crafts. If we'd sneak off together once everyone else was in their bunks."

Just like here. With a chuckle, Asher presses their cock into her hand. She strokes over their wet length, Asher's hips rocking as her eyes stay transfixed on where they fuck her fist.

"I wondered if we'd do this," she murmurs. "If you'd fuck me in the showers, or by the lake, or on the canoes."

Asher groans deep in their throat. "I would have fucked you on every surface," they laugh. "I would have made those corny fucking bracelets."

"I thought about you at football games." Rowen twists her hand around the head of their cock. "Wondered if we would wander off under the bleachers. When I got my first job, I thought about what it'd be like if you came to visit. You'd tell me not to take shit from my boss. You'd tell off my creepy coworker at the holiday party." With a pensive smile, she drags her tight fist over them. "When I got my first apartment, I *wished* you'd show up at the door. I prayed for it, even though you couldn't have known where I was."

It twinges in Rowen's chest, but Asher looks even more mournful, their mouth dipping at the corners. Rowen presses closer to them.

"And every time I had to go home to my mom, I thought about you sneaking into my bedroom." It was the one thing that got Rowen through those visits — picturing Asher scaling the tree outside, slipping through the window and curling up behind her in bed. A wet laugh escapes her; the thought of Asher as a 'winter fling' is laughable. She imagined them in every season. "After the last night, I thought about us running off somewhere. I didn't know where we would go..." She lifts her gaze to Asher's. "But I wished I had gone with you."

When Asher finally kisses her, it's everything. Not the shy, uncertain press of lips from years before. This is whole and deep, desperation and inevitability that makes Rowen's toes curl into the rug. "I would have gone with you," Asher breathes against her mouth, walking her back next to the Christmas tree. "I would have gone anywhere with you."

It sounds like regret. There's a melancholy in their eyes warring with something else before they turn her away and press her chest to the side of the stairs. Asher works the sleeves of her clothes off her arms and drag the rest of the thermal to the floor. Rowen's fingers curl around the staircase spindles, and Asher binds her wrists in place with the ribbon.

"Stay like this," they strain, forehead pressed to her shoulder. "If you keep looking at me, I won't be able to..." Their fingers dig into her hips, making her arch back against them as their cock slots between her ass cheeks. Slowly, Asher rocks against her as if they're hypnotized.

Her thighs tremble, but Asher is imbued with a control she can't place. Powerfully, they loom behind her. Shadows stretch across the staircase, fireplace casting abstract patterns above her. It looks like branches extending from Asher's head, but when they press their nose to her neck, there's nothing but the two of them.

A whine slips through Rowen's teeth when Asher drags their dick against her clit from the back.

"So fucking wet..." They smear slick desire between her thighs before they notch their cock at her entrance. They don't sink deeper, no matter how she shudders. Instead, they flick the ribbons dangling from her hands. "Such a precious fucking present..." They tighten their fingers around her wrists, holding her to the staircase. "Now show me what a perfect mess you can make."

Rowen barely has time to gasp before Asher sinks to the hilt, hips grinding against her ass. It's so good. It's *so fucking good* to finally have all of them, their bare chest pressed against her as she takes everything they'll give.

When they rock forward, she pushes back, desperate and needy. Asher slows, holding Rowen's hips in place as she tugs against her restraints.

"You'll get it, princess." They tug back on her hair until their mouth hovers in her periphery. Slowly, they stir their cock inside, pressing sinfully chaste kisses against her cheek. "You have to chase what you want, right? Then fuck me back like you want it. Work yourself on my cock. Show me how you spent all those years without me."

A whimper wrests its way out of her, but Asher doesn't give in. They keep their hand in her hair, resting their forehead against her cheek to watch where their bodies meet. All she can do is circle her hips back, rolling in a rhythm that feels utterly filthy as Asher hisses.

"That's fucking it. Keep showing me, just like that..."

With every rotation, she takes them deeper, grinding the base of their cock back between their legs. Asher groans, soaking in pleasure as they brace one hand against the stairs.

"Did you play with your sex toys like this and think of me?" Their smirk turns into teeth digging into her earlobe. "In your big girl apartment, when there was no one else to see what you got up to...did you picture me fucking you the way you wanted?"

It makes her legs tremble how they read her so easily. She remembers that night. After everything was moved in, she'd locked the door behind her, drunk on the freedom of a whole place to herself. Somewhere she could be as loud as she pleased, where she could take her time with herself, where she could get herself off exactly the way she needed to.

"Tell me." Asher stirs their fingers against her clit, making her hips buck. "Tell me how *bad* you were that first night on your own. How exactly did I fuck you when you didn't have to hold back any longer?"

Rowen whines in the back of her throat. How does Asher know these things about her? How do they understand her, even after all these years? Things that feel confusing and ephemeral are solid and steady in Asher's hands. They grasp her stifled desire and call to it, like another animal howling in the forest.

There's something hungry and wild inside her, something that's been starved for too long as she tried to live off of scraps. No one else has been able to feed this part of her. She has *always* wanted more. She has always wanted things she can't understand, emotion so deep she can't climb out of it, messy and sticky and overwhelming.

She has always wanted *this*.

It screams through her as if she might combust, fingers curling around the spindles until they creak. "I was..." Her voice wobbles, eyes clenching shut at the sweet sting of humiliation. She's never said it aloud, never put voice to the things she pictured but could never have. "I tried — holding the toy in my hand, but it wasn't right. I couldn't get..."

Asher grabs her hips, guiding her back until she takes their cock completely. "Couldn't get it like *that*?" They bottom out inside her again. "Couldn't get it deep enough? Couldn't make it stretch you out just right?"

A pitiful sound dies in her throat, back arching as Asher holds her in place. Her entire body heats at the words that spill from her. "I had to put it on the floor, just so I could —"

She can't finish the thought, mind reeling as she pants. Asher licks the sweat slipping down her neck. "Yeah? You were thinking about bouncing on my cock even then?" In their voice, the thought is so filthy, making her cunt clench. They hold her tighter as if they can feel it. "How many times did you make yourself come?"

God, it's *humiliating*. She still remembers it — the hot nerves in her stomach fluttering up into her throat. The painful arousal, so sharp she thought she'd combust from a single touch to her clit. The guilt that wasn't strong enough to stop her, but it made her lock her bedroom door just in case. She spent hours on herself that night, playing out every fantasy of Asher that sprouted in her mind. She *ached*. She couldn't stop. "Until I couldn't keep going. Until my legs were shaking too much to hold me."

"Wild little thing," Asher growls against her ear, thrusting their hips again. "And I would've fucked you just like that. Until you couldn't walk. Until you couldn't *stand*. If I'd shown up on your doorstep, you wouldn't have even had to ask. Just one fucking look..." Their hands travel down her body, molding against her breasts and curving over her hips. Then Asher shifts their weight, pushing her up onto her toes so they can drag at a perfect angle.

It makes her eyes roll back.

Asher tugs her hair back to see her face. "Is that it?"

They repeat the motion, making her whimper when they

hit the same spot again. "Oh my *God*..."

That sets Asher off like nothing else, their pace increasing as they drive in deeper. "That's fucking right. It's *me*." Their fingers close around her throat, burning hot as if the ink might sink into her skin.

Their motions are impossibly fast and controlled, driving in deeper than she ever imagined. There is no more restraint; Asher has let go of some part of themself, smashing the wall between them until everything is open and hungry and demanding.

They keep a tight circle on her clit, ripping a sob from her throat. "That's — *fuck* — right there —"

"What?" Asher pants through the exertion. "What's gonna happen if I keep fucking you right there?"

Heat tears through Rowen's body, so sharp and visceral that she can't move. She can't *think*.

"It's ok," Asher simpers. Rowen can do nothing but shudder as they edge her higher and higher. "Come on, princess. You gonna come?"

Her mouth opens, but only a pitiful cry escapes out as she races toward the peak.

"No, you're not..." Asher's hips slow, their fingers stilling on her clit. Her entire body throbs with frustration, a scream threatening to break out of her when Asher leans close again. "Not until I tell you that you're *mine*." Their voice shifts into something untamed, and she swears the ground shakes beneath her. "No matter where you go after this, you're still mine. You've always been mine. You're always — gonna — fucking — be — *mine*."

Every word is punctuated with a thrust of their hips, driving her dizzyingly close to the peak. She clenches her eyes shut, trying to make herself believe their agreement. *Make the most of our few days, right? Then we go back to our lives, no matter what happens here.* But Asher's words are true, even if

Rowen can't have them because she's too fucking scared to *stand up.*

A sound breaks between her lips. Asher swallows it, licking into her mouth like they're reckless for the taste. "And I'm always gonna be *yours.*"

It's the closest they've ever come to admitting it, what Rowen desperately wanted to hear all those years ago. Asher's voice is pained, like they wish they were saying the words back then, before time slipped away.

It takes no more than that. Helplessly, Rowen clenches around them, crying out as her orgasm races through her. Asher buries their mouth against her shoulder, dragging blunt teeth into her skin. That feels like its own release, their body imprinted against her as they take everything she has.

Eventually, the waves of pleasure subside as she drifts back into her body. Asher's hips stroke slowly in and out of her until they withdraw with a bereft hiss. Gently, Asher mouths against the mark their teeth left in her, unwinding the ribbons from her wrists and massaging over her sensitive skin.

It's too easy to sink back into bed with them. Too easy to let them wrap their arms around her, tracing patterns against her bare skin. She doesn't shut her eyes, afraid she'll miss even a second of this as she braces herself. Tomorrow, she will leave. She'll fulfill her duty to her mother, because that is what a good daughter would do. She'll go back to her life, because there is no other option. Because she and Asher agreed when she got here. Because after all this time, neither of them have learned from what tore them apart.

Asher's mouth moves against the top of her head, so soft she can barely hear it. "I can't keep you here. I'm sorry. I can't ask you to stay."

A tear slips to the corner of her mouth, but she's not sure who it belongs to. "I know." Because no matter how close they've gotten, Asher will never let her close enough.

Maybe there isn't a wall between them at all. Maybe it's a chasm.

Twenty-One

Asher

Neither of them want the night to end.

No matter how painful it is knowing tonight is the last, the thought of losing a single moment hurts worse. They lay in silence, Rowen's breath too tight and stilted to be asleep. Once the sun rises, her weight settles against them. Asher runs their fingers through her hair as her body softens, and she dozes off.

Finally, the tension leaves Asher's body. When they're the only one awake, it almost feels like this is one of their hopeless fantasies. Christmas lights glow beside them, the scent of cookies still fresh in the air. If they close their eyes, they can pretend this is just another of their late night thoughts. There will be no pain when it ends. They can revisit this moment as much as they like, and it will feel just the same. *She* will feel just the same. Just as real. Just as warm...

At least, so Asher tells themself.

The thought is so intoxicating they don't realize when it pulls them into sleep. Only the cold, wet press of Bard's nose rouses them hours later. It must be after noon by now. From their bedroom comes a routine beeping.

Mournful realization daggers through them, returning full force at the sight of Rowen still pressed against them. Carefully, they edge out from beneath her and tuck the blankets tighter around her. Let her hold onto the bliss for a little while longer.

Quietly, Asher moves into the kitchen to find a voicemail on their satellite phone.

"Hey, Asher. I tried to get up the mountain this morning to pick up your friend, but your piece of road doesn't seem like it's melted at all. I couldn't even get up there on my snow tires. Anyway, if the ground's that cold, the lake should surely be frozen. Maybe you can cross it and meet me at the fork? Give me a call back if you want me to drive back up."

Fuck. *Fuck.* Asher cards a hand through their hair, panic coiling around their throat. How can the road still be covered? It should at least be driveable. They're this close to getting Rowen to safety, and now...

They have to get her out of here by nightfall. Hurrying back into the living room, they kneel on the mattress, brushing her hair back to wake her. Their chest twinges as she stirs, bleary-eyed and beautiful as her eyes land on them. For one blessed moment, a smile drifts across her lips before reality sinks in again. Her face falls. She remembers last night and what today is.

"Hey..." Asher murmurs, brushing their thumb across the curve of her cheek. Just one more time. Just once more, so they can remember it. "My friend's coming to pick you up. I have to check the lake first. Do not leave the lodge until I come back for you, ok?"

Solemnly, she nods. Asher curls a lock of her hair around their finger, trying to memorize exactly how it feels. It's too much looking at her like this in their living room, the fantasy Asher clung to only hours before coming back to sink its cruel teeth into them. They force themself to their feet, tugging on their clothing and heading toward the door.

"Asher..."

Their eyes slip shut, hand on the doorknob. The waver in Rowen's voice breaks their heart, but they try to keep their expression composed when they turn back to her.

She sits on the mattress, tucked back into her clothes from the night before. Her fingers fidget with one of the sleeves. "Can I ask you something personal? About...your name."

Sweat pricks along their back as their throat dries. They hoped she hadn't noticed, that she wouldn't put the pieces together. Their voice is a sad attempt at casual. "What about it?"

"Why did you pick it?" Her lips press together, as if she's holding something back. "Why did you choose 'Asher'?"

Their heart twinges painfully, as if a fist is closing around it to tear it from their chest. They might as well; it's always going to be with Rowen. Their hand tightens on the doorknob, voice low and quiet. "You know why."

"Tell me," she whispers, pleading for more, just like she did a decade ago. "Please."

The explanation lodges in Asher's throat. *Because everything else in my life was ruined. Because I wanted to be closer to you, even if you were gone. Especially if you were gone. Because rowan trees are called mountain ashes, too.*

Asher can't say any of it, as if the words are trapped in that long-faded night from Asher's memory. As if Asher missed their chance and will never be able to say what they should have.

"Don't run from me." Rowen lifts onto her knees. "Please don't —"

"Because I'm in love with you."

The confession surprises them both. Rowen's eyes widen as Asher releases the breath they've held for the last ten years. Those are words they've never spoken aloud, only written on paper, jarring and powerful and a relief to finally give to her.

So they give her more.

"I've been in love with you for ten years. I know it took me too long to say it. *Way* too long. You were right; I was scared, and it cost me...*everything*." The realization steals their breath like a blade between the ribs. "You are the one thing that I want, and the one thing I can't allow myself. Every night, I wish I could be with you, and every day..." Asher shuts their eyes, remembering the haunted mountain beneath them. "I have to remind myself why I can't."

God, no matter how it feels to say, the words change nothing. That's the most painful piece of it all. Maybe if Asher had told her this back when they should have, things would be different. The two of them could have been brave together. They could have rewritten history, they could have altered everything...but that's not what happened.

"I am in love with you, Rowen..." Asher lets the phrase linger on their tongue, savoring it for a final time. "But I can't have you."

It hurts to say it. It hurts, because it's *true*. When Asher looks at Rowen again, her mouth opens to fight it, but she doesn't know. She doesn't understand. She *can't*. How can they explain it to her?

"This place is cursed," they finally grit. It's as close as they can get to the truth. "*I* am. And I can't keep you here, so please, just...stay inside."

Before she can say anything else, they pull open the door and step out into the snow again.

Their heart races as they tear away from the lodge. It's been years of keeping those feelings inside, and they finally come spilling on the day Rowen has to leave? On the one day a year Asher is forced to reckon with why they can't be with her?

With a string of curses, they shove into the barn and try to start the ATV. There's nothing but a resounding *click*. Brows knit, Asher cranks it again, but the vehicle is silent. Fuck. *Fuck!* How can everything be going wrong at once? Fear claws its icy way up their spine, but they clench their teeth and start off on foot.

They just need to check the lake. With every yard, they glance toward the sun, as if keeping a close watch might prevent it from setting. Their logical mind nips at them. *This isn't going to work. There's not enough time. The fork's too far to walk. Why are you still going?*

But they can't accept it. They can't just lie down and wait for the Wild Hunt to begin, thrusting Rowen into the center of this chaos. What will she think if she sees it? Sees *them*? A sickening feeling swirls in their stomach at the thought of her face, the soft look she gave them this morning dissolving into horror.

Their head snaps sharply. *No*. That can't be the last image she has of them. If nothing else, they want her to remember the past few days the way they do, one final bright spot in their story.

It can't be anything more, but at least it can be that.

They've been playing pretend since Rowen got here. Asher has known that truth almost as long as they've wanted the impossibility of her. A life like this isn't possible for them, because they are monstrous. If they haven't always been that, then at least since the day —

I am not the enemy.

The Voice slips into their thoughts like a second stream of consciousness, making Asher stumble. The Voice feels more potent now, as if it's found every crack in Asher's foundation, flooding in and nearly drowning them in its presence.

The only thing stronger is the pain of their tattoos burning like a brand. Asher clenches their fists. "Then what are you?!"

Birds scatter in the distance, sending dingy feathers fluttering to the ground. It's like a mutilated snowfall, all the wrong shape and color and size, because this forest is fucked up. Because this *mountain* is fucked up, and Asher is at the heart of it.

The Voice strains as if Asher should understand. **I am you.**

They lower their head, barreling deeper into the forest. *You're still my enemy.*

The thought echoes in Asher's mind. Only once the words fade into silence does the Voice whisper, **There it is.**

Asher squints against the pain building at the center of their skull. Before long, that pain will spread and engulf them — but not yet. They still have time. There has to be enough time.

The lake appears in the distance. Asher's strength is renewed, air puffing from their lips as they sprint down the hillside. It must be frozen through. Maybe they can hurry. Maybe they can figure out what's going on with the ATV and get Rowen back on the road...

When they reach the lakeshore, they lift a heavy rock to their chest. Once they test the thickness of the ice, there's still time to get back to the lodge. If they let the Voice out just enough to carry them, they can make it back in half the time, and then —

Asher jolts when their foot breaks through the ice to the water below. It sloshes coldly around their boot, lapping as if it's laughing. Asher can only stare. This has to be a fluke. They pull back, glancing up and down the bank. There has to be a sturdier part of the lake. Shifting around the rim, they find a trusty spot of ice near a tree, gripping a branch and extending their boot toward the ice...

It breaks through the surface again.

Nausea rolls in Asher's stomach. No: they refuse to accept it. This isn't possible. The ice should at least hold their body weight, there's no way...

Further from the shore, the ice is covered in snow. A hopeless panic flutters in Asher's chest, grasping for anything to keep them grounded. It's just the shore that's weak. The center has to be thicker. It's been days, and the snow hasn't even melted on the roads.

Arms weak, Asher swings back and tosses the heavy rock toward the center of the lake. It crashes straight through and sinks to the bottom.

"Fuck!" Asher pants, watching their options melt away before them. This isn't *possible*. The lake was half-frozen last week. There's no way it could thaw that fast, not under these conditions. Not without something like —

Anger spreads through Asher like cracks through the ice, building to a boil. *You did this.*

This time, the Voice's silence is not pensive — it's guilty. But its presence does not waver, as if it's proud of itself. As if it's not ashamed of what it's done.

Another sickly, curling thought occurs to Asher. *That's why the bridge collapsed, isn't it? That's why the bear came to the cabin. That's why there's still fucking snow on the road!*

My power is strongest near the Wild Hunt. The Voice doesn't cower. **I must use what little I have before it fades.**

Why?! Asher storms along the bank, the searing pain of their ink giving way to fury. *To keep Rowen here? To seize your chance to fucking kill her?*

At her name, the Voice nearly purrs. **I love your little heart. How she says my name. How she gives herself**

to me. What a wild little thing.

Asher halts in the snow. A sour taste rises in their mouth, the familiar words seeping across their tongue, like a memory they were only half-awake for.

Do not fear, the Voice murmurs. **I will be gentle with her when the time comes. I already have been.**

It's a truth Asher tried to deny. Last night, the overwhelming heat wasn't just from Asher and Rowen. There was something else there, watching, waiting, clawing its way out whenever it could. Asher wasn't careful enough, too distracted at having Rowen in a way they'd never allowed themself. Of course the beastly Voice was there, salivating and pawing at the cage of Asher's body for a chance to sink its teeth into her.

You've given me a taste of her, but I require more, the Voice rumbles. **You understand my need.**

A chill darts through Asher, their eyes clamping shut to will the thoughts away. *No, I don't. I hate you.*

One begets the other. You do not hate me, you hate your-

Asher hisses in a breath, digging the heels of their palms into their temples. *Why won't you fucking* leave?! Pain splices the center of their skull. *You destroy everything! You make me do things, say things,* feel *things that I don't want. I wasn't just some empty husk before. I wasn't some vacant body for you to inhabit —*

You asked me here! the Voice snarls, pounding like a hammer against an anvil. **You asked not to be alone! You asked not to need the love of another. You asked not to fear your mortal body, for the strength to shape it as you desired. I gave you all of that.**

Asher's skin pulls tight, like too much is crammed inside their body. As much as they hate it, the Voice is right; this is what they asked for. The Voice ensures they are never alone. It consumed so much of Asher's life, they could no longer allow themself to need Rowen. It turned them into such a terrifying beast, they no longer shied away from their human body. They sculpted and carved it into what they wanted, without shame, without fear...but the Voice has made things a thousand times worse.

I am trapped inside this vessel, just as you are. The Voice pulls back from the surface of Asher's body, as if it's trying to compromise. **That cannot be changed, but the mountain does not have to suffer. Magic can return.** *Life* **can return.**

The spell's condition thrums through Asher's pulse. *This place will decay until you let the hound consume your heart.*

I know she is the heart, the Voice urges. *Your* **heart. She cannot leave until I devour her.**

Crushed, Asher sinks to the ground beneath a tree. Already, the Wild Hunt is taking its toll and sapping their energy. It's exhausting fighting the change. Soon, it will overtake them. The Voice will splinter out of their skin and wrest away control. Every creature on the mountain will follow Asher's scent to see what they have to offer the curse.

And if the Voice gets its way, the beasts will only find Rowen.

Asher's head knocks back against the trunk. The sun sinks lower. An ache spreads through their bones, piercing them with pain they can hardly breathe through...but they laugh, a pitiful, hiccuping sound.

The Voice shrinks back from it uncertainly. **It's only a matter of time**, it reassures them both. **The change is coming. I will do what I must.**

Sweat slips down Asher's throat as they smile. *You think I spent...the past decade without her...because I fucking enjoyed it?* Shakily, Asher gets a hand beneath them. When they stumble to their feet, the tree shudders under their weight, knocking snow from its branches. Asher's fingers dig into the bark. *I have kept her from you...for ten years. I deprived myself of her — just so you couldn't get close. Just so she couldn't see what I've become. You think I suffered without her — just to let you destroy her?*

Something howls in the distance. Asher's breathing grows labored as they shed the coat from their back.

She is my heart. You were right about that — but she hasn't been home in years. I locked her out to keep her safe from you. This is nothing compared to that misery.

All those years Asher spent hiding, trapped on this mountain with only the memory of Rowen to keep them going.... Pain jolts through their limbs, threatening to snap them in all the wrong directions. Asher can barely see through the searing pain, but a single thought of Rowen is stronger than anything the Voice does to them.

I will never let you have her. Asher keeps the vision of Rowen at the front of their mind. *Every animal in the forest will tear me apart before you get near her.*

Maybe that's what Asher has to do — allow the wolves of the mountain to swallow them whole, sink their teeth into Asher's beating heart until this place returns to the way it was.

Agony shrieks against Asher's temples. **You will not throw yourself to the beasts! You will not keep the mountain in purgatory! You will not raze both of us!**

Other howls join the first, lost in the fog cascading over the hills and headed straight for Asher. In the distance, footsteps stampede over the ground, growing closer and closer.

With a sickening crack, Asher's body revolts, ripping and tearing as they scream into the wind. The sound twists into something wounded and feral. Control slips from their grasp, but they lunge for it, wrestling with the Voice inside them. It batters their body, like two beasts snapping their teeth as they tumble over a cliffside, too honed on the battle between them to realize the certain end they're plummeting toward.

White-hot pain sears from the edges of Asher's vision. At the top of the hill, the beasts begin to descend, and Asher braces themself.

I will do what I must.

Letter #1

Rowen,

I guess this is goodbye.

That's not true, is it? "Goodbye" was the last time we spoke — or the last time we fought, I guess. We didn't say the word "goodbye," but I'm sure it was for you. You're probably home with your mom now, hating every moment and still smiling like a perfect angel. Or maybe you're with that guy she wanted to introduce you to. Perfect holiday romance, huh?

I bet he doesn't wash his hands. I bet you have to say something three times before he listens. I bet he'll forget to buy you green tea at the store, but you'd still rather be seen with him than me.

Sorry: I'm bitter and angry. Not at you — not really. I've started to understand why you couldn't tell your mom about who you are. What you are. Whatever. I just have a lot of fucking feelings and nowhere to spit them out except this letter.

I went to your cabin the morning after we fought. You don't know that part. Before the sun was even up, I opened the door and whispered your name and knelt by your bunk, but it was stripped. The blankets were gone. The drawers were empty.

Norling told me later that you tried to leave in the middle of the night. She said you were sobbing too hard to talk, and she begged you to stay until you calmed down, so you slept on the living room couch. By the time she woke up, you'd already left. You'd prepped everything for the farewell breakfast, of *course: mixed the pancake batter. Brewed the coffee. Set the table. Because you wanted to make things easier for her. Because you always want to make things easier for everyone else.*

I'm so sorry I hurt you like that, Ro. If you'd been in your cabin that morning, I was going to apologize for everything. I was going to say what I couldn't the night before. I was going to tell you what you knew I felt, even when I couldn't admit it to myself.

You always know me. Maybe that's what scares me, being known like that. Maybe that's why I pushed you away.

I wish I could take it all back. I wish I could go back in time and tell you everything instead of running away...but I did something so much worse.

I don't know what I was thinking. You know I don't believe in that magic shit, but I didn't know what else to do. I didn't want to be alone. I didn't want to be without you. I didn't want to be confused or unhappy, and I didn't want to deal with the gaping hole of losing you. I just wanted some relief.

I didn't really think anything would happen. Norling let me stay another night, and I thought I'd take her scrapbook to the gingerbread shop and get drunk and cry, but when I did the spell, something happened. Everything happened. Looking back, I can barely put the pieces together. I was lighting the last candle, and there was an explosion, and smoke, and pain. God, the pain. When I opened my eyes, my body wasn't mine. I thought the blast had blown me apart, but that wasn't it. No, the spell had turned me into some...thing. Some animal. Some horrifying beast.

I know it sounds delusional. I wish I was fucking delusional. I don't even know what happened after that. All I remember is running and running, fur flashing through the trees.

It took all day to get my body back to itself. Norling was at the shop surveying the damage. I didn't want to see her, to admit what I'd done, but I couldn't run any more. My body just gave out. She took me back to the lodge, and the truth just spilled out of me.

That fucking spell scrapbook survived the fire. I don't know what witch came to cut down a Christmas tree over the years, but they owe me fucking big time.

See? You can laugh. That's what I'm doing so I don't cry. I still feel delirious...and guilty. So fucking guilty for how I hurt you, and how I hurt Norling, too. I burned down the shop. I ruined her memories and hard work because I was weak, just like I ruin everything.

Look at that: my parents were right.

If you were here, you'd tell me that's not true. You'd help me figure out what to do, and you'd make me feel like I'm not a miserable failure for destroying everything I care about. You'd make me feel like I'm not a monster.

But you're not here.

I have to clean up the mess I made. I shut off my phone. I can't go back to my apartment. I don't think they rent to werewolves or whatever the fuck I am now. Norling offered to let me stay at the lodge, but I made her swear not to tell you where I am. She hated to do it. I think she only agreed because she feels guilty, since the spell came from her scrapbook, but I told her it's not her fault. It's mine. It's all my fault.

And I think...I think I might have fucked things up even more than I realized. I found an old fox in the woods yesterday. It looked dead, but it was still moving. Still walking around, like a zombie. From a distance, you couldn't tell anything was wrong, but when you see it up close...

I have to figure out a way to reverse this. I have to find a way to fix it, because if I don't — I'll never be able to see you again. It would be too dangerous. I would be too dangerous.

Even now, I can tell there's this part of me that's...ravenous. A gaping pit that craves things, like an animal that hasn't been fed in years.

I can't send you this letter. I'm trying to come to terms with that, like it might make this whole thing easier to deal with. If I brace myself for it now, it won't hurt as much when it happens. I don't think it's hit me yet, what it means for us if I can't fix this. I'm going through all of the memories we won't get to make. We won't get to live together. We won't get to see each other in spring and summer. We won't get to visit the farm when we're too old to chop down trees anymore.

Fuck. Fuck. Bracing for it doesn't make it any easier. I think it's starting to hit me.

Happy fucking New Year.

— I'm not sure how to sign this.
  I'm not sure who I am anymore.
  I'm not sure what I am.

Twenty-Two

Rowen

Something is wrong.

Rowen paces the kitchen in the fading light. This isn't the first time Asher's vanished, but they said they were coming back. They said they would take her to the lake to catch her ride down the mountain, but there's been no sign of Asher since.

Just stay inside.

It's what they told her since the beginning, but something odd is happening in the forest. She can't put her finger on it, but it's like the quiet mountain is suddenly thrumming with activity. It's a feeling more than anything, the sense of something beneath the surface, like a beehive or an anthill. Bard recognizes it too, whining and pawing until Rowen peers out the window.

Flocks of birds fly overhead as deer bound through the

trees, snow shaking from branches as squirrels skitter across. It's like all the animals are running from something, pointed through the forest toward the lake.

Rowen's stomach flips. She needs a drink. Once she makes a cup of tea, Asher will be back, and she can stop worrying. Her hands haven't gotten the memo, still trembling as she pulls open drawers and cabinets. Where are those teabags?

She tries to remember the first day, with Asher in the kitchen and her waiting awkwardly in the foyer. Asher bent down for something... She follows the motion, crouching in front of the sink and pulling open the cupboard. That can't be right, though. Underneath the basin, there's nothing but cleaning supplies and boxes...and something stuffed into the back corner.

Its vibrant ceramic peeks out from a pile of rags. Stretching, Rowen reaches it and pulls it into the light. The curved "R" of the handle is familiar under her hand. The mug is the same bright red-orange, the color of rowan berries that she spent weeks replicating. Her fingers brush the ragged edges of her name carved into the bottom. There are a few more chips in the glaze, the inside of the mug stained from years of use. In the decade since she left it behind, this mug has been well-loved.

Light vanishes from the bulbs overhead, draping the lodge in darkness. Bard yips, scurrying back and forth in front of the windows as Rowen searches for a flashlight. The power must be out again. She tries to stem her rising dread, but there's no fire in the hearth, just shards of moonlight cast through the windows. It's full tonight, ominous and heavy.

Outside, the animal cries grow louder.

Bard scratches at the front door. "I know, boy." Rowen does her best to sound soothing, but her voice is tight. Where is that flashlight? "We just have to wait a little while..." But she's not convincing herself. Hand over her eyes, she cleans the glass to see if she can make anything out.

Shadows dart past the cabin, creatures flying through the snow. She sucks in a breath as they chatter and howl as if they're on the trail of something.

Asher.

No, she tells herself. *It's something else. A wounded animal, or —*

Behind her, something snickers outside the kitchen. Bard snaps at the sound, nails scrabbling across the hardwood as a shadow passes over his dog door. Rowen yelps, clenching her teeth and snatching Bard into her arms as she races upstairs.

She slams the staff closet door behind her, fumbling in the darkness to press her ear against the wood. Has the creature managed to get inside? It's impossible to tell with the animals blurring by outside, their calls bouncing off the lodge. Even from this window, their bodies are lithe and limber, darting across the snow as if they're chasing something.

God, *where is Asher?* She sinks hopelessly to the ground, something clacking under her heel. Bard's ears perk, nose lowering to investigate the old floorboard knocked out of place. Her sweaty palms wipe against her pants. *Ok.* She steadies herself. *Maybe there's still a shot of alcohol in there.* That's all she needs, a little liquid courage so she can figure out what to do about Asher. Shakily, she pries the board away and reaches into the gap.

Paper rustles under her fingers. Brows knit, she withdraws and peers down into the hole. There are no bottles, only folded papers that fill the entire space. What *is* this? It doesn't matter. She needs to focus on Asher. She needs to figure out what to do, but something gives her pause. Strange sensation spreads through her, drawing her to dip her hand back into the crevice. When she unfolds one of the papers, Bard noses at her hand as if he recognizes the scent.

Rowen,
I guess this is goodbye...

It's Asher's handwriting, the page discolored with wet spots. Rowen's breath catches in her throat, eyes racing over the words as if she can't read them quickly enough. Emotions gather into a puzzling mess in her chest. What starts as bittersweet tenderness dissolves into a whirl of confusion.

Magic? She tries to reread, but there's too much to take in, her brain whirring to comprehend. It's...unreal, mind flooded with images of fire, fur, and that scrapbook of spells.

Frantically, she digs out another handful of paper from the cramped space, as if it might provide some other explanation. Every letter is addressed to her, spanning the last decade.

Year fucking two...
It's the fourth year since you left...

She can't even begin to skim them all, but fresher ink catches her eye.

I don't think I can take much more of this. It's my ninth Christmas Eve under this curse. The Wild Hunt is starting, like every fucking year. I can hear the animals coming. They'll hunt me all night, and all I can do is run from them, but sometimes I wonder what would happen if —

A shriek pierces the air. Rowen clamps her hands over her ears before she recognizes the tone. It trills in her pocket until she tugs her phone free.

Incoming Call: Mom

Rowen's grip tightens. She'd forgotten about the reception

in this room. Gnawing her lip, she glances out the window, where dusk has faded into night. She needs to do something. She has to do *something*, even if she doesn't understand exactly what — but maybe her mom can send help.

Clenching her eyes shut, Rowen presses the phone to her ear. "Mom, something is —"

"Don't start!" Even through garbled static, her mother's voice is furious. Rowen's stomach sinks. "I've — waiting *days* — couldn't even call? What kind of daughter —"

The rest is lost to static. Rowen tucks her knees toward her chest, pressing a finger against her other ear. "Mom, there's something dangerous —"

"I don't care!" Those words come through loud and clear, a stinging strike that makes Rowen flinch. "Do you know — wasted waiting on you? How this makes me look? — should be ashamed —"

Gritting her teeth, Rowen rests her head against her knees. It's easier to let her mother talk. That's why her mother's so wound up; she hasn't had Rowen to take her anger out on. Her mother will run out of steam. She always does.

But Rowen doesn't have fucking *time* for that. There's a rising fire in her stomach as she lifts her voice. "I got stuck. I got snowed in, but I need help right —"

"Don't talk over me!" her mother snaps. "Always an excuse! — not sure I even want you —"

Rowen's nails dig into her palm. Her mother's only saying it to hurt her. That's all. But — fuck it. It *does* hurt. "Fine." Rowen swallows. "Then I won't come."

"I knew — avoiding me!" It's dizzying how her mother changes tactics. "You never even wanted — did you? Sorry — so miserable for you — woman who birthed you, fed you, *raised* you. Sorry I'm such a *terrible* mother."

Frustration vibrates through Rowen's limbs, but it's not solely for her mother. It's for *herself*. Has she really sat here and taken this for the past ten years? For *longer*, an entire life of clamping her mouth, bowing her head, trying not to inconvenience anyone else? Just like the day she left this mountain, when she agreed to meet some pointless boy to keep her mother happy. When Rowen threw away her own life. When she lost Asher.

Stand up, princess. Their words nudge the back of her mind. *Chase what you want, or catch what you're afraid of.*

"You *are* a shitty mother."

Rowen's voice sounds unreal, even to her. The other end of the line goes silent, and then, " Excuse me?"

Satisfaction heats Rowen's cheeks. "You're right." The shock in her mother's voice strengthens Rowen's. "You are a horrible, miserable person. All you do is criticize, and all I do is try to make you happy."

Rowen gets her feet under her and rises back to her full height.

"I don't want to visit you for Christmas. I don't want to take care of you. You know what? I don't even want to talk to you now." Who knows how bad the static is? It doesn't really matter if her mother hears it; it matters that Rowen says it. "I'm fine, by the way. I'm alive, at least. Until today, I was — fucking great, actually." Her mouth burns at the curse, high on adrenaline, and she relishes in the feeling. "I'll keep being great if you don't call me again."

She clamps down on the power button, letting the phone fade to black before she tosses it onto a shelf. Her blood races with renewed purpose. Whatever is out there, whatever this curse or spell has created, she will not let Asher face it alone any longer.

She's going to find them.

Jerking open the door, she and Bard race down the stairs. Moonlight casts across the portrait on the wall: a hound and stag lying together, the dog licking the deer's wounds.

In the foyer, she tugs on outer gear before she finds the flashlight on the windowsill. With a gloved hand, she pets Bard between the ears and tugs open the front door.

Wind rushes into the living room, slamming the door back against the wall. With all her strength, Rowen grabs the rifle and pulls the door shut behind her. Even with moonlight, her eyes strain to adjust to the darkness. A thick cloud of fog has settled on the mountain. She glances furtively around the cabin; there are no more moving shadows, only trenches and footprints headed in the same singular direction.

A twig snaps in the forest. Her head whips toward the treeline. *Just the wind*, she tells herself, eyes lowering from the stinging cold. *It's just the wind.* But the tops of the trees do not sway, and the rest of the hill is silent.

Her flashlight sweeps across the snow as she continues to follow the animal trails. Tiny chipmunk paw prints are lost under the pads of foxes, all drowned out by meaty paws with five long claws. She swallows cold air, tilting her flashlight into the depths of the trees. Her beam does little to pierce the darkness, but this is where the trails all lead.

She glances back to the lodge. It's almost invisible through the fog, but its shape stands dark and silent, the same way it must have looked all these years. The same way it will be if she doesn't find Asher. Chin pressed down into her scarf, she parts the curtain of pine needles and steps into the forest.

It's so much darker beneath the branches. Snow hardly reflects her flashlight as she stumbles through the undergrowth. Outside the hat pulled over her ears, the forest sounds are muffled, keeping her body tense as she edges along.

Branches rustle overhead. Her flashlight whips toward them, but she can't make out more than a bushy tail. Something's off about it. Her eyes narrow before she realizes the fur is lopsided, a chunk missing from the side, glowing wet and bloody under her light.

Her stomach turns. *The animals aren't right. When you see them up close...* She presses her scarf against her face to hide her breathing, easing forward until her boot catches on a fallen log. The rifle clatters against her back. Her hands swing out to catch her, losing their grip on the flashlight that knocks against a rock. With a *clang*, it topples into the snow and peters out, leaving her in nothing but darkness.

Twenty-Three

Rowen

A low growl builds a few meters away.

Heart thudding, Rowen searches frantically for the flashlight until her gloves land on something solid. Trembling, she knocks against the side until the flashlight sputters back to life. From the depths of a bush, an eye reflects back at her. It prowls slowly toward her, a mountain cat baring its teeth as it emerges from the fog.

The cat's throat rumbles, and Rowen can see the vocal cords vibrating. Light glints off a second eyeball hanging from its socket. Rowen wants to heave, but fear keeps her frozen. Ribs poke through the cat's fur, mottled yellow bone piercing slippery pink skin. One leg is almost completely bare, bony feet staggering through the snow.

The flashlight flickers out again. Breath shallow, Rowen slams her hand against the side as the sounds of the animal draw closer.

In the blackness, she jerks the rifle off her back. Her finger trembles near the trigger, using only her ears to aim. What if she misses? What if she hits something else, like Asher? What if this creature *is* —

An eerie silence falls over the brush. Rowen hears nothing over her pulse. With her eyes clamped shut, she prepares for impact — but it never comes. When her eye cracks open, the flashlight flutters again, casting light up to the branches overhead.

She almost doesn't look; she knows what she'll see. Light catches on glistening eyes, one pair turning into dozens of others. A scream catches in Rowen's throat. Owls and bats and birds all stare down at her, their heads cocked at the same angle. Decay spreads through all of them, fur and skin sloughing off, holes exposing bones and organs.

Rowen clamps a hand over her mouth. This isn't real. It *can't* be real, it isn't possible —

If only.

She's not sure what sets the animals off — the voice or her scream. Treetops shake with the sudden departure, squawks and screeches tearing off into the night and leaving her alone again.

Alone except for the voice.

That wasn't Asher's voice. She presses her lips together, stretching toward her flashlight. Who else could be out here? Could they help her, or do something far worse?

When she closes her fingers around the flashlight, it stutters out with a terrifying finality. Rowen shoves her hat up over her ears to listen, but she can't make out anything beyond distant wind and yips of a coyote.

Light appears in the distance. Rowen opens her mouth to

call out, but she shuts it fast. What if the voice isn't friendly? What if it belongs to someone worse than everything out here? What if —

Icy fear crackles up her spine at the realization. The voice can't be human. She hadn't spoken anything aloud — the voice answered a thought in her head.

Across the snow, the light draws closer, hauntingly blue and shimmering like the aurora borealis. Rowen presses closer to the ground, ducking behind the tree stump in front of her. Maybe it won't see her. Maybe she can...

But the light follows a straight path to her, diffusing through trees and fog. Antlers branch from its head, neck extending to a bulky body and delicate deer legs, a stag made entirely of light.

It holds its chin high, casting light across the snow. There's something...divine about it, magical and majestic. It's not quite a deer, either; a wolfish tail swishes behind it, its body a strange combination of gentle hart and burly carnivore. Only when the creature comes to a halt does she realize it's looking directly at her. Its eyes are frosty white, but she swears there's a smile on its lips when the voice comes again. **How I have waited for you.**

Her heart jumps into her throat. The stag's mouth doesn't move, yet the words envelop her with warmth. She doesn't know what this creature is, but it feels so familiar, like a reunion with someone she hadn't realized was gone.

Her breath puffs into the chilly air. "What..."

The stag lifts its head higher. **I am the Guardian of the Mountain. The Horned One. The Living and Dying God.**

Shakily, Rowen forces herself to her feet. This is...impossible, but the stag glimmers before her, transparent and still very real.

I have used the last of my magic to meet you here.

Our time is short. The stag flinches at something in its mind. **My vessel is split. It has never rebelled against me this strongly; I tried to get it somewhere safe.**

Uncertainly, Rowen remembers Asher's letter. Is that why she found it? Because this — magic encouraged her? "Is this because of the spell? Do you know where Ash-"

They called to me for aid, and I provided. The creature's eyes darken. **But my magic comes at a price. I drew from the mountain to give them what they asked.** The stag tilts its head toward the trees. **You've seen the creatures and the forest. We are trapped in this state: dying, but never dead. We exist like this until the magic is repaid.**

"Repaid by Asher?" Rowen isn't sure if it's a threat, or a deal, or something more ominous. Her fingers close around the rifle barrel. "I'm looking for them. I need to find —

I. Am. Asher, the stag bellows. It takes a step toward her, and she tries not to shudder. **We are one and the same; we cannot be extricated. We are two trees from the same root, two tines from the same horn. No matter how they bury me, I do not die.**

Something warm flutters in Rowen's stomach. Her eyes widen as she tries to snuff it out, but the stag seems to sense her puzzling flicker of desire. It lumbers silently across the snow, drawing ever closer.

I became what they fear. The part of them that hungers. The part that does not flee. The stag stops in front of her, lowering its head until it hovers above hers. **The part that *needs*.**

She sucks in a breath when she shivers. She does know this creature. It was there the night on the couch, last night against the wall, its antlers spread in shadow across the stairs. Her body recognizes its pull from the wanton way Asher gripped her, the certainty with which they took her, the possessive mark of their teeth into her skin.

I have been denied, the creature growls. **I have never been fed. I have been left unsatisfied...**

Something presses solid and warm against her back. In her periphery, a shadow towers above her, but she can't turn her head to look. Hot fear makes her head swim, but she bites back a groan when warm breath curls against her ear.

"I have been *starved* of you."

For the first time, she *feels* the voice. Her head whips beside her, but there's nothing but stark absence. Trees rustle in the distance, like wind dispersing through the bush.

Even as I became that gaping pit, maw open and crying out, I could not fill the absence you left in them. The lighted stag circles behind her. **I have heard their thoughts of you. Yearning, desperate, clawing deep in their bones.**

Rowen whimpers, thighs clenching as the stag's snout nuzzles her ear.

It was enough to make me *crave* you, too.

Her knees threaten to buckle. In the distance, a pack of animals cackle, and the stag lifts its head.

The forest is restless tonight. It is the only time the creatures can hunt the one who holds our magic. *The Wild Hunt*, Rowen remembers. The stag nods as if she has spoken. **But there is a way to release our power back to the mountain, to return life to this place. Do you know it?**

She remembers the spellbook, Asher's handwriting scrawled across the page. *Until magic returns to the mountain. Until our two paths converge. Until you let the hound consume your heart.* "What does that mean?"

The mountain needs balance: the changing of seasons, the circle of life and death, the predator and prey... The stag's lips spread in a smile. It's a haunting look, unnatural and inhuman, but its teeth are even stranger. Long canines extended from a sharpened row, like the mouth of a wolf rather than a deer.

Rowen steps back, tripping over the rifle strap.

Do not fear... The stag licks its teeth, and Rowen shudders at fear and arousal conflicting within her. It's as if she wants this creature to sink its teeth into her and take a bite. **Over the cursed years, my essence has warped to give the mountain what it needs. Balance, predator and prey — but it is not what I'm meant to be.**

The stag stops moving toward her, closing its mouth as it tilts its head like a gentle doe.

Asher spoke to me. They said something I hadn't considered... The stag circles her appraisingly as she tries to keep it in sight. **My arrogance assumed I was the hound, the predator, the hunter...** Sharpened teeth flash as the wolfish tail flicks. **And since your arrival, I thought you were the heart. Vital. Precious. *Delicious.***

Rowen stumbles back against a tree, gloved hands against the bark trying to keep herself upright.

But Asher locked you out of their heart. That's what the spell was meant for all those years ago, even if the effect was muddied. The stag stops before Rowen, pride in its gaze. **You are not meant to be consumed, wild little thing. It is *you* who must consume *us*.**

Sweat breaks out beneath Rowen's layers, her mouth falling open for a long moment. "I'm not..." *Hound consumes the heart.* Her head spins, voice dazed. "You have the wrong idea. I'm not — part of some prophecy. I'm —"

You sought them out the season you met. The stag's eyes glow brighter. **You hunted them for years. You tracked them to this mountain without even knowing. You chased them into this wilderness. You follow them, no matter how they hide. What will happen**

when you catch them?

Rowen's teeth chatter, and she doesn't know if it's from the cold or something else. Something bigger. "I'm not a hound; if anything, I'm..." *A rabbit. A bird. Skittish. Fragile. Weak.*

Mirthfully, the stag shakes its head. **Loyal even when you ought not be. Eager to please. Willing to put yourself in danger for one you love. You are growing into your fangs, little Hound.**

Rowen shivers under the realization, tucking her arms across her chest. Is it possible? Could she do more than cower and wait? Could she finally, *finally* get what she's been after? It sounds like a hope she never dared let herself wish for. She shakes her head. "I can't hurt Asher. I won't. I won't...consume them. I won't — *eat* them."

A fond smirk slips across the stag's face. **Perhaps it's not meant in the animal sense. Perhaps to consume their heart is to fill it, overwhelm it, captivate it.**

It's how her heart has felt for them all this time. If Asher's letters are true, if they let her in...

You are not alone in your hunt, the stag assures her. **You remember the picture: the hound chasing the stag?**

In her mind, she looks down on the drawing from the book, but the picture rotates. Now, she sees the purpose of the circle. While the hound chases the stag, the stag follows in return.

Asher may have run from you, little Hound. When the stag steps closer, she doesn't back away, her gaze locked on its glowing eyes. **But I have been hunting *you*.**

A whine builds in her throat as the stag lowers its snout to her neck, warm breath over her racing pulse.

We understand each other, you and I — wanting, and never fulfilled. Its tongue drags over her throat.

Desiring, and always denied.

Heat coils between her legs, her eyes slipping shut as snow dusts her cheeks. Her voice is breathless. "You want me to —"

It does not what matter what *I* desire. Firmly, the stag pulls back. **You must choose your path, and serve no one but yourself. The mountain will not accept your answer unless it comes from you alone...** Somberly, the stag averts its gaze. **And the mountain will know. After my...near-mistake, I owe Asher this.**

Snow melts on her eyelashes, wind beginning to swirl around her. "And if I give my answer? If I offer myself, what happens?"

I cannot say for sure. Somberly, the stag settles its weight. **Magic causes changes; nature will tip the scales to return its balance. Your body may shift, as Asher's has.**

It's a sobering thought. Who knows what that would mean for her? She still doesn't know for sure what Asher has struggled through on their own...but deep down, there is no question. If it means being with Asher, she'll do whatever it takes. She *wants* to. For the first time, her desires are within reach, and she refuses not to chase them.

Will you hunt? Snow gusts around them as the stag's light scatters through the fog. **Will you leave your cage and devour us?**

Rowen reaches for the creature, but it slips between her fingers like its whisper fading on the wind.

Find me, little Hound, if you choose to sharpen your teeth.

Twenty-Four

Rowen

As soon as the stag disperses, Rowen's flashlight flickers back to life.

Its beam sweeps the ground as she runs, shoving branches aside and leaping over fallen limbs. Her movements are no longer hesitant, eyes honed straight ahead as she breaks out of the forest.

The fog is already clearing. At the top of the hill, she slides to a halt and stares down the long rows of Christmas trees. It's impossible to imagine this place used to be a festive wonderland. In the dark, the trees are thick and overgrown, hiding god knows what behind them. A few meters down, something darts between the foliage and makes her tense — but only for a moment.

She is the Hound. She does not need to cower. She has made her choice.

Shoulders squared, she slips down the hillside, bracing against trees as she stumbles through snow. There are animal tracks beside her leading to the burnt-out wreckage of the shop. This is where Asher performed the spell, magic so powerful it destroyed the building itself. This must be where the Horned God brought them to keep them safe.

When Rowen reaches the base of the hill, she sucks in a breath. Animals of all kinds surround the wreckage, as if they're waiting for something. For *her*. As she approaches, their faces turn toward her, minks and lynxes and wolves rotting before her. Her heart trips over itself. After a long moment, the animals clear a path to the burnt cabin door. Cautiously, Rowen steps forward. The creatures do not lunge for her, rotted eyes following as she passes. Only when she reaches the charred door do the animals move again, slinking back into the forest with their haunted eyes on her.

Wind rushes down the mountainside and blows the cabin door open. It's dark inside the wreckage, roof tilted and full of holes where snow and moonlight enter. There is no furniture left, just the remains of wooden counters that lead into the building's depths.

A grunt echoes from the distant dark. On the ground before her are a set of prints, smeared hooves mixed with hands that lead to the back of the building.

Fear flutters in her ribcage, but she sets her jaw. She won't go back to the lodge, or the person she was before, or her life without Asher. With one slow step, she crosses the threshold.

Deep in the building, the noises stop. So does Rowen, boots sinking into the snow before a voice thunders through the darkness. "*Get out of here, Rowen!*"

The voice is both Asher's and not, familiar and strange, like an imitation of the person she knows. It sounds like Asher and the stag warring within the same body.

Rowen grits her teeth. "I'm not leaving you."

Despite her trepidation, it feels good to say it. Her feet are firm beneath her. Above the howling wind, the creature growls. Rowen thrums with a curious emotion, hot one second and frozen the next, cold sweat breaking out beneath her clothes.

"I'm not leaving you," she says again, mustering conviction into her voice. "I'm not going back to my mom or my life. I'm staying with you."

Hooves scrape the floorboards. "You *can't*," the voice strains. "This is — a horror — no one should have to face."

"Are you no one?" Her body thrums with energy. It feels good. It feels fucking *amazing* not to sit meekly behind, not to duck her head and do as she's told. "It's been ten years of this, hasn't it, Asher? You've been dealing with this alone."

The voice doesn't respond.

"I understand the spellbook now. I read your letters."

The voice hisses, lumbering closer to her in the shadows. It's three times the size of Asher, avoiding the pool of moonlight on the floor.

Rowen swallows. "You don't scare me," she whispers.

The creature stops. Its head tilts before slowly, it steps into the light.

The Horned One is truly the living and dying God. Its head is a deer skull without fur or eyes, two empty sockets peering down at her. Antlers extend from both sides of its head, intertwined with holly and twigs from the forest. Its teeth have the same sharpened points she saw on the stag moments ago, furry tail flicking behind it.

But the creature before her now is a mixture of animal and human. Beneath the deer skull is Asher's neck and torso, glowing pale beneath the tattoos Rowen traced her fingers over. Aside from Asher's arms and hands, there is no more of their human body. The trail of hair on their stomach leads down to the four-legged body of a deer, like a centaur with a deer skull for a head.

Even in shadow, it's clear the deer body is half-alive, ribs exposed through patches of fur. This creature isn't decaying; there's no smell or festering wounds or infection, but it's trapped in the same near-death state as the rest of the mountain.

Steam puffs from the skull's nose. "I *should* scare you." Asher's hands gesture down their body, deer legs trembling as if they're using all their strength to fight themself. "You asked for my worst. This is it, this...*thing* that I've become. Dangerous. *Vile.*"

"Not to me."

Asher shakes their head, foliage slipping from their antlers. "I will accept nothing from you. I will *take* nothing from you."

"You're not taking anything." Without a thought, Rowen's hand darts out to grip Asher's arm. "I'm *giving* you something. I'm giving *myself.*"

A wounded sound escapes Asher. "You don't know what that means." The skull stares mournfully down at where she touches them. "What you're agreeing to. What you'll be stuck with."

Asher could extract themself easily from her hand...but they don't. A powerful feeling surges through her. "You," she states plainly. "That's what I'm after. That's what I'm hunting. Now *stop running from me.*"

At the promise in her voice, Asher groans. It's a terrifying thing to face such devotion. She knows they're tempted to snap their jaws, to sprint away and lick their wounds in solitude.

But for the first time, Rowen sees herself as she is: the Hound, the balance, the other half of the scale. This is the path she's always wanted to follow but been too scared to take the first step.

She isn't afraid anymore.

"The mountain requires an offering." She tugs down the zipper of her jacket. "I'm here, and I'm willing...God of the Forest."

A snarl rips from Asher's throat, hooves pawing the ground as the deer body lowers to its knees. The hollows of Asher's eyes burn hot as coals, scorching away any chill in the air. "You can't talk to it like that, Rowen. It wants you."

"I'm talking to *you*." Her jacket falls open, spilling off her shoulders into a heap on the snowy ground. "*All* of you."

Asher digs their hands into the snow, fighting the needy creature inside them. "I can't — stop it. I can't hold it back."

"Then don't." She yanks the laces of her boots undone and toes them off. "I told you, I want all of you. Every part. Every iteration."

Asher laughs painfully. "You would give yourself to a God?"

"I would give myself to you."

The muscles in Asher's arms flex as their head hangs, fighting with the part of them that wants to crawl toward her. There's a long moment of silence before Asher speaks again. "You're doing this for me. To help me."

Rowen tugs off the rest of her clothing, wincing at the static before she leaves them all in a makeshift-blanket on the floor. Hair raises on her arms, goosebumps spreading along her bare skin as she steps toward Asher. "I want to help you, because I love you. Because I want to be with you. Because I've spent so long without you, and it just makes everything...less. Less happy. Less real. I'm less of *myself* when I'm not with you. This is for me, too." Her hand traces the skeletal line of their jaw, lifting the hollows of their eyes up toward her. "I made my choice. No matter where you run, I will follow. As long as it takes."

Asher shudders through their final resistance before they

lunge, taking Rowen to the ground. She sprawls across her clothing, panting as antlers scrape on either side of her. Asher's skeletal mouth drags along her body, smearing its scent against her. Marking her. *Claiming* her.

Even in Asher's desperation, they rest their head between her hands. "You've caught me, Hound." Their look is a blazing mix of carnal softness. "I will not run any longer."

Rowen whimpers at the voice. It's no longer a distorted impression; it's a mixture of Asher and the stag together. It's Asher, but hungrier. Asher, finally opening their mouth to be fed. Asher, as a God.

They mouth against her hand, taking each finger one by one between their skeletal jaws. An inhumanly long, warm tongue worships every inch of her palms. Heat swells between her legs, her naked body exposed to the air as the God pins her between its antlers. She takes Asher's head in her hands. "Show me how hungry you've been. Let me feed you."

With a vicious growl, Asher digs their antlers deeper into the ground. "I will honor your offering." They nudge her knees apart with their skull, lifting her legs with their hands to drape her thighs over the base of the antlers

A whine crawls up her throat, torn between blistering heat and freezing cold when the God lowers its mouth. She arches off the ground, helpless to escape the cage of its antlers. Its tongue drags against the juncture of her thigh before it smears against her clit.

She grips the antlers. "Ash..."

Asher shudders as her fist curls around one of the spires, hips rutting as if she were wrapped around Asher's cock. Human hands dig into her thighs, lifting her ass off the ground so Asher can angle deeper. They never ease off her clit with the base of their tongue, sinking the tip inside her. She grinds against Asher's mouth, whimpering through the deliciously foreign stretch. The God's tongue reaches deep, pressing against the needy spot inside her as it rolls against her clit. Legs trembling, she clenches her eyes shut as her sudden release drags her over the edge.

"I've waited years to remember your taste," Asher laps at her core, groaning low in their throat. "My memory does it no justice." Removing her legs from its horns, the God prowls up her body.

"More," she gasps. It's the only thing she can say, the only thing she wants. *More of you. More of every part.* Asher drags the flat of their tongue up her sternum, completely covering the place between her breasts. Rowen's head spins, a dog with its first taste for blood. "*More,*" she demands.

Asher laughs against her throat. "You think you can stand it?" Between Rowen's legs, something teases her thighs, thick vines curling and twisting from the deer body. "Being taken by me? *All* of me?"

It's as if the mountain itself desires her, dead leaves falling from Asher's antlers to rest on her breasts. When the leaves touch her body, they crackle and bud back to life. Asher watches in awe, fingertips tracing the outline against her skin.

"Nothing has bloomed here for so long..." Asher whispers, a glimmer of their human self pressing to the surface. Yet they wait for Rowen, as if she can withdraw and return back to the safety of the lodge.

But Rowen is as hungry as they are, twining Asher's fingers with hers to bring their human chest against her. She drags her teeth over their shoulder. Asher ruts between her legs, pressing the tattooed rowan berries to her mouth.

Headily, she sucks a bruise against them, curling her tongue in filthy patterns that make Asher groan. Vines coil around her calves and ankles. They jerk her beneath the furred body, keeping her legs lifted as the God settles its forelegs over her. "Look at you, little Hound..."

A whine spills from her like the animal she is, hair splayed and body flushed, writhing beneath Asher like a creature who's been caught. A vine curves up her thigh, brushing between her legs while other flora bloom to keep her in place. Snow filters in from the hole in the ceiling, gathering in the greenery of the antlers. When Asher tilts their head, flakes fall onto Rowen's bare chest, making her gasp as the vine pushes inside her.

Asher lowers their mouth, licking the stinging cold patch from her breast. It's a shock to her system, temperatures clashing, making her squirm at the mix of pleasure and pain. Asher's mouth closes over her breast, trapping the cold against her skin before their warm tongue laves her painfully peaked nipple. When Asher's mouth withdraws, a gust of air assaults the wet track they left behind and makes Rowen cry out.

Then Asher shifts forward, aligning their hind legs between her thighs as the vine pumps into her. When the God rocks its hips, the vine sinks deeper, making both of them groan as if the appendage is part of Asher themself. They hang their head, shuddering as their hands clench into the ground above her.

Tempestuously, Rowen swirls her hips. "Oh, ancient God: is one mortal pussy too much for you?"

With a growl, Asher bottoms out inside her, so deep and sudden that Rowen gasps in pleasure. "Only yours." Asher stirs inside her, their groan clamoring to the surface. "Only ever yours." When Rowen's eyes roll back, Asher lifts her head to force her eyes to find theirs. "Look at me. *Look at me* when I give you what you asked for."

A helpless sound breaks through her lips, but Asher gives her no reprieve. She clenches around the vine as the God grinds its pelvis against her clit.

"One more." Asher lowers their head, the hollows of their eyes honed on hers. "Give me your offering. *Let me have it.*"

With a stilted cry, Rowen comes apart again, shivering around the vine. Asher doesn't slow, rolling into her through every wave of her orgasm.

"Little hound...princess..." With every motion, the vine sinks deeper. The God's pace increases, hips meeting the back of her thighs as it works her toward the peak again. "Wild little thing."

Her nails dig into the snow, a whimper pitching into her throat. "You said one more —"

"Have you known a God who isn't greedy?" Asher laughs. "Have you known a merciful God?" The vine stays inside her as the furred body backs away, kneeling to allow human hips to settle between her legs. When Asher and Rowen's bodies roll together, the vine rocks deeper. Asher lowers their mouth to her throat, human chest dragging against hers. "You have followed me. Hunted me. Caught me." Asher twines their fingers together, pinning her hands above her head. "Now consume me. *Devour* me. Take all of me. I have only ever been yours."

Release tears through her, her sounds spilling into a sob as she digs her teeth into Asher's chest. Blood blooms from the inked berries above Asher's heart. It stirs something inside Rowen — something *wild*. Her lips press to the mark and draw blood into her mouth while Asher groans in pleasure. Enraptured, they watch as dark red smears across her face, her clenching cries peaking against their skin.

Only then does Asher finally, *finally* give her all of them, burying themself inside and toppling into their own release.

Once both their breathing slows, Asher allows her hands to slip from the restraints. Carefully, she cradles Asher's skull against her neck and laves against their wound. Just like the portrait from the lodge, the Hound lies with the stag and laps the pain away.

Slowly, so slowly, the vines withdraw. Snow drifts to the ground around their bodies as the forest settles into blissful silence. Fur and bone and antler recede, until there's nothing but bare human skin pressed against Rowen. It's the Asher she's most familiar with, but not the Asher she loves any more than the other.

The two of them stay intertwined, chests rising and falling as the heat between their bodies keeps them warm. Asher shifts between her sore legs, setting their elbows on either side of her head as they brush sweat-slick hair back from her face.

Their look steals her breath. Where she has always found care and passion, she now finds something open and unguarded, God and mortal converged into one. When they look at her, there's new depth to their eyes.

Twice the intensity. Twice the adoration. Twice the untamed love.

Epilogue

Asher

Five Years Later

Today, the height of spring breathes life into the mountain again. It is no longer trapped in its decaying state. Flowers bloom beneath sapling trees as newborn wildlife stumbles onto fresh legs.

Bushes and branches disguise Asher's antlers, their nose lifting when they catch Rowen's scent. She's sneaky, but not nearly enough to escape Asher's senses. Not when they spend innumerable hours at her side, so familiar with her smell that they can taste it.

Not when they've spent the last five years hunting her.

A quarter mile away, Rowen is nearly silent as she slips into a pond. Asher gives chase, hooves carrying them swiftly through the forest. They give Rowen a wide berth, circling in front of her patch to catch her off guard.

Her eyes stay peeled behind her, searching for Asher through the trees. When Asher collides with her, they both tumble through the brush in a tangle of laughter. Asher keeps their prisoner captive, pinning her beneath their stag body.

These days, the Horned God is both easier and harder to contain. It no longer feels like a separate entity, but a part of Asher themself. The God no longer claws to escape Asher's human form, but shifting now is...freeing. The wolfish parts have fallen away, returning them to their deer shape. Sometimes, Asher inhabits the stag completely, without a trace of their human self. Other times, like now, they sink back into the centaur mixture Rowen saw on Christmas Eve all those years ago.

No matter their shape, she still looks at them like she desperately wants to catch them.

Underneath them now, wolf ears peek out from her hair. Her body has gone through changes, too. Whenever Asher transforms, she shifts right along with them.

The more you embrace it, the better it gets.

"Are you done running, princess?" Asher winds their hips between Rowen's thighs. Her breath becomes a whine, but Asher can't help teasing. "If this is too much, you could always go back down the mountain..."

When she smiles, her teeth are as sharp as her claws digging into Asher's hips. "I'm never going back."

It doesn't surprise Asher. Every day is better than the last. With each passing season, Rowen grows lighter and more certain, as if the mountain is reclaiming what always belonged to it: her spirit. She is no longer shy about who and what she is. When the two of them visit the reopened shops along the mountain road, she holds Asher's hand and leans into their chest, a rainbow ribbon in her hair.

From the field around them now, she plucks an unbudded flower and weaves it into the fur at Asher's waist. Under her touch, the petals bloom, much like everything else on the mountain. Much like Asher.

"What about you?" she asks cheekily. "Are you done running, O Horned One?"

No longer does she have to wonder; Asher tells her their needy, hungry truth. The barrier Asher built around themself did more to keep them hidden and small than it ever did to protect them.

Asher cradles her face in their hands, running their thumbs over the freckles on her cheeks. "Not done running after you."

She leans her cheek into their touch, hair spilling through the flowers. The pads of her fingers brush their chest, tracing the berries and the tiniest scar hidden among them. "I love your every iteration."

Asher brings their forehead down to hers, pressing a soft kiss to the corner of her mouth. "I wrote you another letter."

Her smile spreads against them. "Will you read it to me?"

Humming, Asher melds their lips to her jaw. "Aren't you tired of my letters?"

"Are you tired of mine?"

Silence falls abruptly. "Touché." They nip her skin to draw out her laugh.

It's become tradition to read through the letters they never sent to each other. Some are frustrating. Some are funny. Most are painful, but the heartache is easier to bear now. When Rowen and Asher are curled up together, reading those old words and tending to old wounds, it feels like looking back on a different life. Still, they cherish every letter, preserving them in the metal tin when the floorboards couldn't hold any more.

Now, Asher and Rowen can write letters whenever they want, and they always make sure to read them.

"I'll read it to you..." Slowly, Asher slots their mouths together, teasing their tongue against her lips. When she opens, they drag their teeth into her lip with a smirk. "If you catch me."

Then Asher is off into the forest, Rowen's shouts echoing behind them as she gives chase once more.

The two of them care for the mountain now, tending to its living and dying. Sometimes, they travel to other places, but they're always happy to return to the lodge and watch the seasons pass. When the mountain grows cold again, they will still be there, chasing each other through the snow. They will mold another ornament from clay and carve their names into the back. Their Christmas tree will be covered in memories new and old, the scent of cider and cookies in the air. They will remember the last time Mrs. Norling came to the mountain, overjoyed at the sight of the lodge and forest returned to their former glory. They will reminisce about her around the bonfire when old friends come to visit. They will make room for Bard to curl up between them, candles glowing in every window and warmth overflowing from every crevice.

The Horned One's path has converged with Asher's. The Hound has consumed their heart, as they have consumed hers. Magic has returned to the mountain.

And this magic doesn't feel like a curse. It feels like a gift.

* * * * *

THANK YOU for reading *Christmas with the Horned God*! **Want more Asher & Rowen?** Sign up for my NEWSLETTER or join my PATREON for extra scenes!

AVEDAVICE.COM/NEWSLETTER
AVEDAVICE.COM/DISCORD
PATREON.COM/AVEDAVICE

About the Author

Aveda Vice is the author of sinful stories and infernal paranormal romances. In her books, you'll find a weakness for monsters and polyamorous pairings. She researches true crime, decorates every day like it's Halloween, and is going to hell.

AVEDAVICE.COM

Sign up for Aveda Vice's NEWSLETTER and PATREON to stay up-to-date on new releases, special offers, and bonus content.

Follow @AVEDAVICE on TWITTER and INSTAGRAM for sneak peaks and promotions.

Join the FANGS WITH BENEFITS FACEBOOK READER GROUP for community chats and posts.

Leave a review for this book on AMAZON and REVIEW sites.

Acknowledgements

I spent months trying to write a story. I drafted three different novels, but I could never seem to finish editing any of them. Then Monster Manor had one of their "Moodboard Mondays," and I thought, "what would a creepy Christmas story look like?" A bit of plot came to me, and when I posted the moodboard, the response was so inspiring. In only a couple months, I had completely finished a story that I love, and that story is *Christmas with the Horned God*. For that, I want to thank you, reader. Any time you are excited by my work, please know that it makes all the difference. I truly appreciate you.

My beta readers gave such wonderful feedback, even in my tight timeframe. Brilliant darling Steph (and cat Nora), the melting grinch Ames, and the immeasurably talented Rien. Without you, this story would not be what it is today.

And thank you again, Rien Gray, for your story *A Strip of Velvet*. It, along with Freydís Moon's *Heart, Haunt, Havoc* and *With a Vengeance*, inspired this story of haunting, possession, and wild spirit. I hope this book does your beautiful stories even a fraction of justice.

Sweet Rabbit, thank you for loving my most prickly edges.

Made in the USA
Las Vegas, NV
30 December 2023

83726840R00125